Once Upon a
Rhyme
Little Voices
From The South
Edited by Helen Davies
& Jenni Bannister

First published in Great Britain in 2011 by:
YoungWriters
Remus House
Coltsfoot Drive
Peterborough
PE2 9BF
Telephone: 01733 890066
Website: www.youngwriters.co.uk

Book Design by Tim Christian

SB ISBN 978-0-85739-343-2

THIS BOOK BELONGS TO

....

Foreword

Here at Young Writers our objective is to help children discover the joys of poetry and creative writing. Few things are more encouraging for the aspiring writer than seeing their own work in print. We are proud that our anthologies are able to give young authors this unique sense of confidence and pride in their abilities.

Once Upon A Rhyme is our latest fantastic competition, specifically designed to encourage the writing skills of primary school children through the medium of poetry. From the high quality of entries received, it is clear that Once Upon A Rhyme really captured the imagination of all involved.

The resulting collection is an excellent showcase for the poetic talents of the younger generation and we are sure you will be charmed and inspired by it, both now and in the future.

Contents

Maddie Stewart is our featured poet this year.
She has written a nonsense workshop for you
and included some of her great poems.
You can find these in the middle of your book.

Winkfield St Mary's CE Primary School, Bracknell

The Poems

Show Time

I'm now backstage,
I shiver and quake,
In a minute it will be time,
To sparkle and shine,
My dream has come true,
For I'll be in front of you.

What if I forget to skip?
What if I stumble and trip?
My legs go weak,
I can't move my feet.

Turn on the song,
I'm now coming on,
Happiness fills my heart,
For the show is about to start.

Saskia Collins (10)
Ann Edwards CE Primary School, South Cerney

Funny Clown

This clown is a very funny fellow
With a big red nose,
And hair that is green and yellow.
Sometimes he makes me laugh,
With goofy clothes and a big tall hat,

He touches his hair,
And squeezes his nose.
He bends down low
And touches his toes.
He jumps up high and twirls around,
And crosses his legs and bumps to the ground.

Harry Randall (11)
Ann Edwards CE Primary School, South Cerney

Gymnastics

I started gymnastics when I was four,
My first event was the floor,
When I finished everyone cheered,
I just stood there standing in fear.

My second event was the bars,
I hoped I could reach Mars,
All the chalk got in my eye,
And it made me want to cry.

Everyone started clapping,
I didn't know what was happening,
A lady told me I'd won,
And to go and see my mum.

I started gymnastics when I was four,
My first event was the floor,
When I finished everyone cheered,
I just stood there standing in fear.

Laura Hallett (9)
Ann Edwards CE Primary School, South Cerney

Autumn

The lovely summer has finished her stay,
And soon little autumn will come to play,
The leaves are dropping to the brownish ground,
And soon little acorns will be found.

The men will soon start to reap,
And little animals will go to sleep,
Feel the wind and smell the pine,
Let's get ready for harvest time.

The wind is strong and really blowing,
And the streams are very roughly flowing,
Pull up a pillow for the tiny creatures,
And admire autumn's colourful features.

Charlotte Hughes (10)
Ann Edwards CE Primary School, South Cerney

Moonlit Midnight

In the
Forest,
There's a
Spooky silence,
Deep in the forest,
There's a tiny dwarf,
Deep in the forest,
There's a deadly
Dragon,
Deep in the forest,
There's a blood-curdling cry,
Deep in the forest,
It's full of mischief,
Deep in the forest,
There's a curious smell,
Deep in the forest,
There's a mysterious sight,
Deep in the forest,
It's a
Moonlit
Midnight.

Sam Brewster (10)
Ann Edwards CE Primary School, South Cerney

Clowns

In the circus,
Scary faces,
Red paint like blood,
More like vampires,
Than acts in a circus,
Smiling cautiously,
Like hungry wolves,
Hats and magic tricks,

This is my huge fear.

Charlotte Mann (10)
Ann Edwards CE Primary School, South Cerney

Noises In The Night

I am feeling sleepy,
'Cause it's 10 at night,
I think I'm going to go to bed,
And wake up when it's light.

I am feeling dozy,
And dropping off to sleep,
Snuggling into my duvet,
Snuggling deep.

I hear a noise,
Coming from the door,
I hear a noise,
Creeping up the floor.

It is out to get me,
Get me to eat,
I am hiding under the covers,
With my teddy, Pete.

It is climbing up the bedpost,
Right next to me,
It's coming up the duvet mountain,
It's lifting up the sheet . . .

I am clinging onto Pete the ted,
With all my might,
I see its greasy, slimy face,
About to take a bi-

My eyes flicker open,
Seeing my mum and dad,
'Are you OK my honey pie?'
'Darling I think you've gone mad!'

Rose Holgate (9)
Ann Edwards CE Primary School, South Cerney

Superstar

I wanna be a superstar,
Bright, beautiful and bold,
I wanna be a superstar,
Until I'm grey and old.

I wanna be a superstar,
And no one can stop me now,
I wanna be a superstar,
And be able to take a bow.

I wanna be a superstar,
I wanna be a superstar
I wanna be a superstar,
The brightest of them all.

Kirsty Price (9)
Ann Edwards CE Primary School, South Cerney

I Heard . . .

It was so peaceful that I heard
Petals fall like
Rain dropping on a tin roof.

It was so quiet that I heard
Someone blink like
Soldiers marching.

It was so silent that I heard
Myself thinking like a
Swarm of bees around a honeypot.

It was so peaceful that I heard
Coral reefs swaying from side to side like
Trees in a hurricane.

Lauren Taylor (11)
Berry Hill Primary School, Berry Hill

Cackling Countries

In France
They do a silly dance
In purple spotted underpants.

In Tunisia
The maths is easier
And the houses are bigger too.

In Bangkok
They have smelly socks
While saying tick tock to their own clock.

In Spain
They drink champagne
While tied to a chain
Hanging from a crane.

In Peru
They have a smelly shoe
And tend to lose it too.

In Wales
They eat snails
While meeting males in
Dirty jails.

Tamara Bridgeman (10)
Berry Hill Primary School, Berry Hill

Desires

I like chocolate.
Like daffodils adore the spring.
Like a pearl cherishes the ocean.
Like a ring relishes a lady's finger.
Like trees admire summertime
I like chocolate.

Amy Hall (10)
Berry Hill Primary School, Berry Hill

In Beijing

In Beijing when the clock
Goes dingalingling they
Wake up and go praise their king.

In Miami
When people go dodally
They like to be called Sally.

In New York
Where people use hands instead of forks
They like to eat pork.

In Greece
When you have a nephew and niece
You're allowed to have a feast.

In Spain
When you're in a lane
It often rains.

In Hollywood
It's like being in the neighbourhood
Where they have dolls that are china and wood.

Bethany James (10)
Berry Hill Primary School, Berry Hill

I Like Chips And Beans

I'm looking forward to chips and beans,
Like a pencil is thrilled by a fresh piece of paper,
Like a kettle is excited by a cold tap,
Like a football is thrilled by the back of a net,
Like a curtain is happy when night comes,
Like a crisp packet likes people's hands,
I enjoy chips and beans.

Kelton Morris (10)
Berry Hill Primary School, Berry Hill

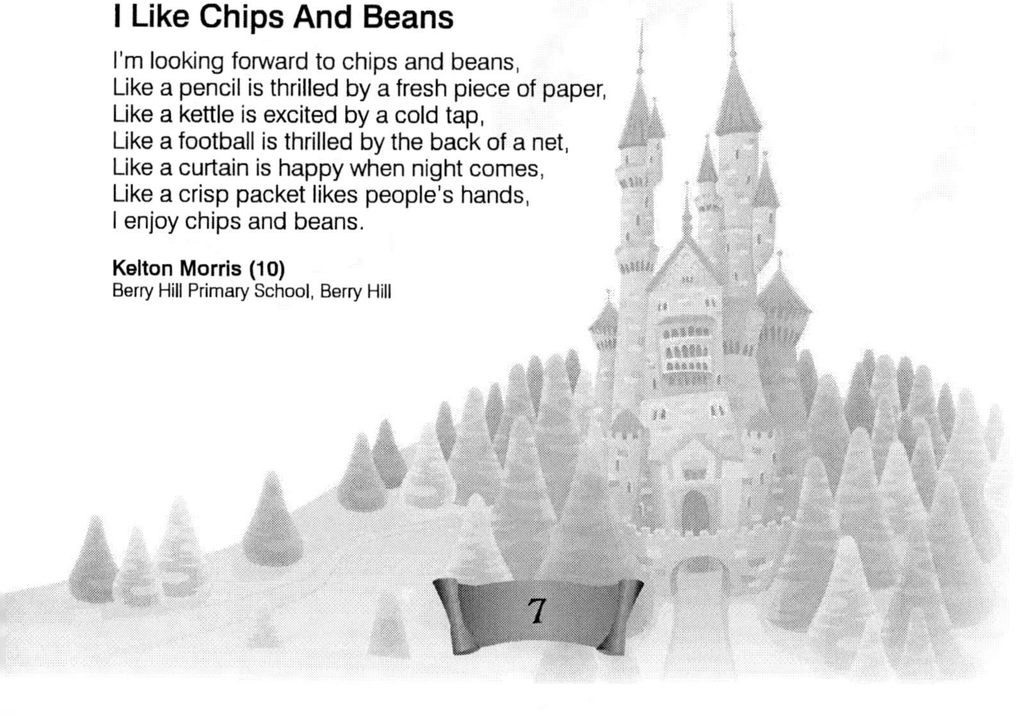

It Was So Peaceful . . .

It was so peaceful that I heard
Grass growing on top of the fresh moistured soil,
Like a thousand doors being slammed shut.

It was so quiet that I heard
Ants carrying tiny crumbs to their nest,
Like people frantically shopping on Christmas Eve.

It was so calm that I heard
The breeze brush past a rose petal and make
It fall onto the cold concrete flooring,
Like an elephant ripping up trees in the forest.

It was so silent that I heard,
A crab's legs side-walking on the beach,
Like an old grandfather clock chiming the hours.

It was so tranquil that I heard
A panda chewing on bamboo shoots,
Like an electric digger cutting into concrete.

Alex Lusty (10)
Berry Hill Primary School, Berry Hill

Fantastic Countries

In Spain I saw a man smoking
In a crane.

In Berlin they have a baked bean tin
To throw in a bin.

In New York they like to eat pork
Off a silver fork.

Someone in Greece has a son called Reece.

People in France like to dance in sexy underpants.

In Delhi they watch telly while eating jelly.

Kieran O'Brien (11)
Berry Hill Primary School, Berry Hill

My Excellent Ears

It was so calm I heard
A bluebird heavily landing on a branch,
Like a piece of rock hitting the ground
After being flung from an erupting volcano.

It was so hushed I heard
Someone rapidly winking,
Like a swarm of a million bees
Buzzing around a hive.

It was so silent I heard
A hungry caterpillar quickly munching
On a leaf
Like a car gulping up the diesel
From a pump.

It was so peaceful I heard
Red fire ants marching
Like a group of children clashing
Cymbals together.

It was so tranquil I heard
A vile mosquito sucking the blood
Of an unlucky child,
Like a cat with a fresh bowl of milk.

Ceri Jackson (10)
Berry Hill Primary School, Berry Hill

I Am Scared Of . . .

I am scared of spiders
Like a mouse is horrified by a cat
Like an antelope is petrified of a tiger
Like a pond is panicked by winter
Like a fish is frightened of a cormorant
Like a leaf is anxious of a rake
I am scared of spiders.

Hannah Goddard (10)
Berry Hill Primary School, Berry Hill

A Pocketful Of Poems

People in New York
Love eating pork
With a shiny silver fork.

Everybody in Berlin
Has a baked bean tin
To chuck in the bin.

Someone in Greece
Has a son called Reece
Who has roasted geese.

People in Jamaica
Have a local baker
And a vegetable maker.

People in Miami
Have a son called Danny
To keep a sheep called Lammy.

People in France
Love to dance
In their fancy underpants.

Wilson Davies (10)
Berry Hill Primary School, Berry Hill

Funny Names

People in Spain
Drink champagne
Whilst on a plane.

People in Peru
Have smelly shoes,
And encrusted loos.

People in Wales
Eat snails
Whilst watching gales.

Boys in Tokyo
Are called Pinocchio
They have lots of jokios.

People in France
Have sexy spotty
Underpants.

People in Japan
Are often called Stan
And don't like ham.

Brooke Belson (10)
Berry Hill Primary School, Berry Hill

Our Wacky World

Boys in Chile,
Are always silly,
And they're called Billy.

People in Vancouver,
Like eating Hoovers,
Also they are groovers.

In Dehli
They eat tellies,
Whilst drinking jelly.

In Berlin
People are thin,
Because they live in dustbins.

People in Iran,
Have a blue van,
They like hugging their nans.

People in Rome
Are always on the phone,
Also they are made from chrome.

Men in France,
Like to dance,
In pink underpants.

Kayla-Mae Skidmore (11)
Berry Hill Primary School, Berry Hill

Spindly Legsphobia

I am scared of spiders.
Like a mouse is terrified of a cat.
Like a tree is petrified of a woodcutter.
Like a pen is frightened of heavy boots,
Like a ruler is nervous of a child's hand.
Like a balloon is traumatised by a needle.
I am scared of spiders.

Libby Amson-Dluska-Miziura (10)
Berry Hill Primary School, Berry Hill

Crackers Countries

In France,
They do a funny dance,
In their underpants.

In Spain
They spill champagne,
And get a stain.

In Peru,
They have smelly poo,
And it tends to get flushed down the loo.

In Australia,
They're a lot lazier,
Than anywhere else in the world.

In Delhi,
They watch the telly,
While eating ice cream and jelly.

People in Japan,
Like the name Stan
And don't eat ham.

Michael Leech (10)
Berry Hill Primary School, Berry Hill

I Heard A Crocodile . . .

I heard a crocodile clapping with his hands,
I heard a nail snoring in the sand,
I heard a camel kicking some ice,
I heard a snowman chatting to some mice,
I heard some cheese whispering, cluck, cluck, cluck,
I heard a chicken yelling
Luck, luck, luck,
I heard a clover leaf
Swooping in the sky,
I heard a cloud yodelling
Bye-bye.

Gabrielle Cackett & Josh McKenzie (10)
Berry Hill Primary School, Berry Hill

Fantastic Facts

In Chile
If you are silly
You get told off by Billy.

In France
People like to dance
In spotty underpants.

In Peru
People like to canoe
And they are all called Sue.

In Cuba
People like to play the tuba
But never go out to scuba!

In Jamaica
They like to bake-a
Big fat creamy cake-a.

In Tokyo
They like to watch Pinocchio
And like to look macho.

Penny Whittington (10)
Berry Hill Primary School, Berry Hill

I Look Forward To . . .

I look forward to a football match
Like a cat is excited about a ball of wool.
Like a calculator is thrilled about a page of sums,
Like a plane is jubilant about a trip to Australia.

Harry Griffiths (10)
Berry Hill Primary School, Berry Hill

Funny Countries

In France
They like to
Dance in spotty underpants.

The girls in Chile
Are so silly
And their names are Milly.

In Cancun
They eat baboons
With coconut macaroons.

The teachers in
Spain always
Fall down the drain
After drinking champagne.

In Delhi
They watch telly
Whilst munching jelly.

Chloe Brooks (10)
Berry Hill Primary School, Berry Hill

Rugby Match

I look forward to a rugby match.
Like a football is excited about being kicked at a football match.
Like a bed is ecstatic about being laid in at night-time.
Like a pencil is happy about being written with on a clean sheet of paper.
Like a rubber is excited about rubbing pencil out when we are at school.
I look forward to a rugby match.

Declan Fissenden (10)
Berry Hill Primary School, Berry Hill

Fun, Fun Facts

In Peru
My dad had the flu
And did not know what to do.

In New York
People eat pork
On a shiny fork.

In the Philippines
They have jeans
And eat beans.

In Russia
I had a bit of blusher
And people like Usher.

In Spain
There is a worldwide plane
Then it started to rain.

Thomas Hedges (11)
Berry Hill Primary School, Berry Hill

Fantastic Poems

In Greece . . .
People often
Like to wear
A fleece whilst
Hugging their niece.

In France . . .
People prance
Around in
Their underpants
And do a
Lively dance.

In Spain . . .
The rain
Travels by train
Which is rather insane.

Lucy Alexander (10)
Berry Hill Primary School, Berry Hill

Countries

In Brazil
People like to burn bills and take pills.

In Berlin
People look thin and live in a dustbin.

In France
People like to dance in their sexy underpants.

In Miami
They look jammy in their pyjamas.

In Jamaica
They had a baker who was a great creator.

The Japanese have dirty knees
And like to eat chillies.

In the Philippines
They have baggy jeans and like to eat beans.

In New York
People like to eat pork on a golden shiny fork.

In Paris
People get embarrassed when they look at a Toyota Harris.

Tommi Peacey (10)
Berry Hill Primary School, Berry Hill

It Was So . . .

(Inspired by 'A Poem to be Spoken Silently' by Pie Corbett)

It was so hushed that I heard
Pretty petals swaying and drifting slowly to the ground
Like dancers jiving in Heaven.

It was so quiet that I heard
Long overgrown grass groaning as it grew
Like an old man getting out of the chair.

It was so silent that I heard
My dog think like a lawnmower
Churning and chewing the grass as it cut.

Thomas Harrison (10)
Berry Hill Primary School, Berry Hill

The World's Most Quietest Moments

(Inspired by 'A Poem to be Spoken Silently' by Pie Corbett)

It was so peaceful you could hear
Seeds popping beneath the fresh soil
Like exploding popcorn going crazy in a hot pan.

It was so hushed I could hear
Autumn leaves falling like huge
Hailstones pounding on a conservatory roof.

It was so quiet I heard myself
Thinking like a concert audience
In Wembley Stadium, roaring
And screaming at their favourite popstar.

It was so silent that I heard
Myself blink like a roll of
Thunder rumbling close by.

It was so peaceful I could
Hear a caterpillar munching
On a freshly grown leaf
Like a horse's hooves
Galloping in twisted lanes.

It was so hushed I could
Hear ants marching with
Their trembling legs like
Rio carnival with
Singing, dancing and celebrating.

Jasmin Elsmore (10)
Berry Hill Primary School, Berry Hill

I Saw A Lion . . .

I saw a lion with a mane of blazing fire,
I saw a flame rise like a midnight choir,
I saw a mynah bird in a cave,
I saw a hairy caveman having a wild rave,
I saw a gorilla singing to the Queen,
I saw a crown jumping over a five foot beam.

Harriet Elsmore & Olivia Edwards-Trigg (10)
Berry Hill Primary School, Berry Hill

Wonderful World

People in Spain
Drink champagne
Whilst on a plane.

In Delhi,
They watch telly,
Whilst eating jelly.

People in France
Have a chance
To do a famous dance.

People in Wales
Eat snails
Whilst watching gales.

People in Legoland,
Step on yellow sand,
Whilst watching Brand and Mand.

Sophie Taylor (11)
Berry Hill Primary School, Berry Hill

Wembley

Climbing up the steep, hard wall
Reaching over the high, hard wall.

Ascending up the gigantic, white Wembley arch
Mounting over the huge, white Wembley arch.

Examining up the slippery Wembley pitch
Viewing over the slidy Wembley pitch.

Strolling up the players' tunnel
Shuffling over the echoing players' tunnel.

Ewan O'Brien (9)
Berry Hill Primary School, Berry Hill

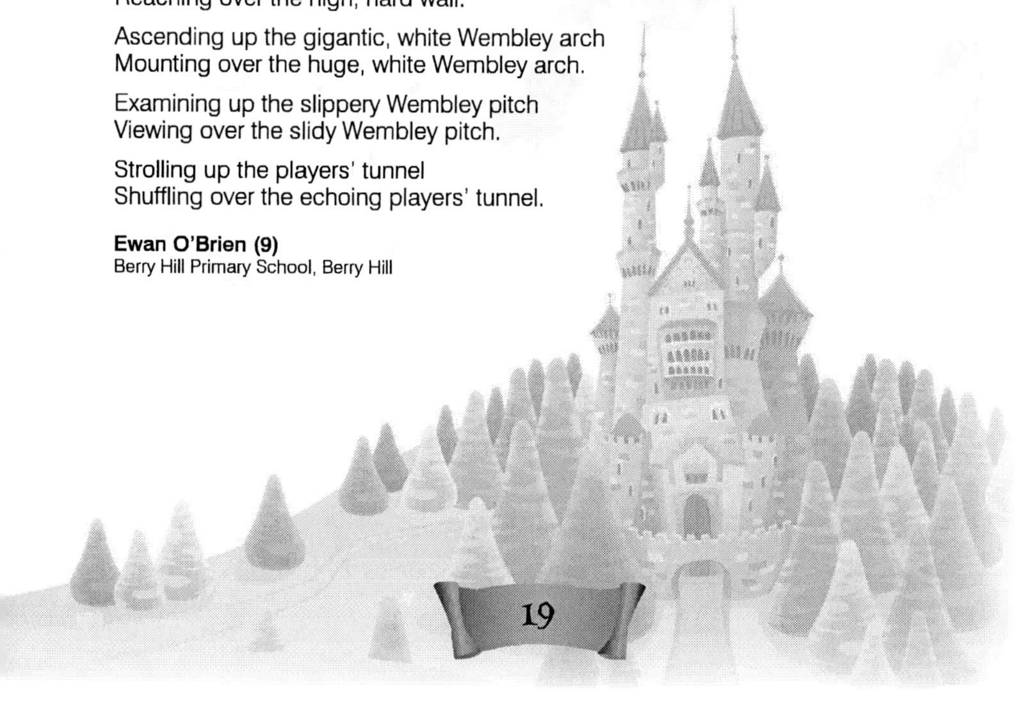

I Saw A Mongrel . . .

I saw a mongrel eating a bed
I saw some pillows filled with lead
I saw some teeth that flew like a bee
I saw a wasp swim in the sea
I saw a beach in the middle of the South Pole
I saw a flag with a picture of some coal.

Charlie Revill & Alexandra Atock (10)
Berry Hill Primary School, Berry Hill

I Saw A Pig . . .

I saw a pig singing to the Queen,
I saw a crown on a runner bean,
I saw a pea on a cat's tail,
I saw a stripe on a blue whale,
I saw water jump on the sun,
I saw fire eating a bun,
I saw some bread do a dance,
I saw a child eat snails in France.

Jacob Smith & Rhys Wintle (10)
Berry Hill Primary School, Berry Hill

I Heard A Pig

I heard a pig singing to a priest.
I heard a church that was talking to the east.
I heard a Chinese man barking to a mouse.
I heard a dragon tail rustling in the house.
I heard a castle tower whistling in the sky.
I heard a bird crunching on an apple pie.

Courtney Harris & Harvey Baldwin (10)
Berry Hill Primary School, Berry Hill

Busy Road

Jogging up the bumpy hill,
Riding over the misty hill.
Running up the dark hill,
Hopping over the brown hill.
Springing up the snowy hill,
Climbing up the snowy hill.

Amy Price (8)
Berry Hill Primary School, Berry Hill

The Beautiful Waterfall

Running up the huge waterfall
Sailing over the huge waterfall.

Hopping up the broken bridge
Skipping over the broken bridge.

Jumping up the dirty fence
Scrabbling over the spiky fence.

Todd Morris (8)
Berry Hill Primary School, Berry Hill

A Wonderful World To Me

Skipping up the yellow flowers
Running over the yellow flowers.

Jumping up the sandy beach
Swimming over the sandy beach.

Climbing up the rocky cliff
Flying over the rocky cliff.

Zoë Hedges (8)
Berry Hill Primary School, Berry Hill

What A Wonderful World

I can see
A light fresh purple flower swaying in the breeze,
Flying seagulls gracefully over the blue sea.

I can hear
Birds tweeting in the bushy green tree,
Fireworks splitting people's ears.

I can smell
Colourful, sweet marshmallows as I walk into the shop,
Honey, sticky and sweet in the bees' hive.

I can touch
The cold sea as blue as the sky,
Dogs' soft golden fur like prickly bales.

I can taste
Candyfloss like a cloud in my mouth,
Chocolate melting like snow.

Abigail Fitton (8)
Buckingham Primary School, Buckingham

A Quiet World

(Inspired by 'A Poem To Be Spoken Silently' by Pie Corbett)

It was so quiet that I heard moles digging under
The mud.

It was so quiet that I heard leaves dropping
Dangerously.

It was so quiet that I heard worms wiggling
Slowly.

It was so quiet that I could hear people breathing.

It was so quiet that I heard sticks rolling.

It was so quiet that I heard sunbeams shining.

Katy Winget (8)
Buckingham Primary School, Buckingham

It Was So Quiet That

(Inspired by 'A Poem to be Spoken Silently' by Pie Corbett)

It was so quiet that
I heard minds thinking all over the world.

It was so quiet that
I heard me blink at night.

It was so quiet that
I heard raindrops hit the ground.

It was so quiet that
I heard blood pouring out of some skin.

Oliver George (8)
Buckingham Primary School, Buckingham

During The Storm

During the storm,
The lightning flashed violently in the sky.

During the storm,
The tornado spun like a spinning top.

During the storm,
The rain crashed like a BMW and a Honda.

During the storm,
The thunder boomed like a rock band at a concert.

During the storm,
The hail was like 1,000 sugar cubes falling from the sky.

During the storm,
The snow fell slowly down on the horizon.

During the storm,
The river crashed violently against the bank.

During the storm,
The sky grew darker as the sun went down on the west.

Joe Clark (8)
Buckingham Primary School, Buckingham

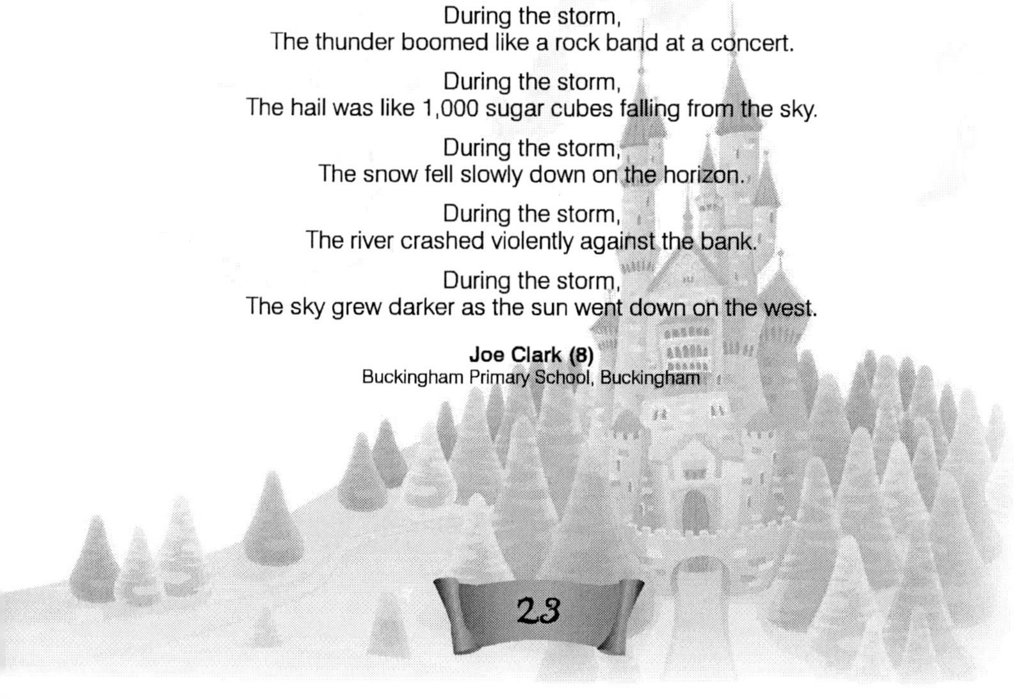

During The Storm

During the storm
The rain rattled
Like horses' hooves
Pounding on the roof.

During the storm
The wind howled
Like wolves whistling in
The moonlight.

During the storm
The thunder boomed
Like a giant
Having a tantrum.

During the storm
The lightning flashed
Like lights being
Switched off and on

After the storm
The clouds cleared and
The shining sun came out.

Lily Viner (8)
Buckingham Primary School, Buckingham

I Can See

I can see

A bright orange sports car
Whizzing speedily down the road.
Stripy monochrome zebras cantering
In the flowering field.

I can hear
A vulcan bomber soaring in the
Bright blue sky.
A tiny puppy yapping excitedly.

Finley Birch (8)
Buckingham Primary School, Buckingham

During The Storm

During the storm
The lightning crashed fiercely
In the sky like a car's engine blowing up

During the storm
The wind whistled wildly
Like a referee blowing his
Whistle

During the storm
The rain thumped on the ground
Like a giant thumping on the floor.

During the storm
The hail felt like stones falling from the sky.

Ben Law (8)
Buckingham Primary School, Buckingham

Storm

Flash!
A strike of lightning lit up the sky
Like a street lamp!

Bang!
Thunder crashed
Like it was angry with the clouds!

Plunge!
The rain pounded down
Like a horse galloping through a field!

Whoosh!
The wind raged like
Animals escaping from a zoo!

Nothing can stop a storm!

Josie Shuker (8)
Buckingham Primary School, Buckingham

Silence

(Inspired by 'A Poem to be Spoken Silently' by Pie Corbett)

It was so quiet that the pens on the white boards
Sounded like a sewer full of rats and mice.

It was so quiet that I could hear the flight
Feathers of a bird rustling in the wind
As it flew over me.

It was so quiet that I could hear myself
Breathing heavily as well as a few other people.

It was so quiet that I could hear a bird
Calling to his mate.

Benjamin Everest (8)
Buckingham Primary School, Buckingham

Whilst In The House!

Whilst in the house the thunder roared
Like two lions fighting over a piece of meat.

Whilst in the house the hail was the size of
Candyfloss at a fair.

Whilst in the house the wind blew frantically
Blowing people off their feet.

Whilst in the house the lightning struck like a boomerang.

Emily Cavender (9)
Buckingham Primary School, Buckingham

During The Storm

During the storm,
The wind was thrashing
Through the bushy trees.

During the storm,
The thunder was
Roaring.

During the storm,
Hail was falling
Out of the bright blue sky
Like a bomb
Plotting down on
The ground.

During the storm,
Rain was crashing
Like a machine gun
Going off.

During the storm,
Lightning was flashing
Energetically.

During the storm,
The clouds faded and everything was peaceful.

Jacob Ballinger (9)
Buckingham Primary School, Buckingham

During The Storm

During the storm
The wind whistled
Like an angry
Referee blowing
His whistle for a
Red card.

During the storm the lightning
Struck like a storming
Fast goal banging in the
Net.

During the storm hailstones
Shot down like a
Rock in the sky.

During the storm the rain was a
Big hard football
In the sky.

Joe Phillips & Zak Momen (8)
Buckingham Primary School, Buckingham

It's A Wonderful World

I can see
My puppy gracefully lying in the bright
Hot sun.
My family laughing crazily at a silly TV show.

I can taste
Chocolate slowly melting in my mouth
Sweets chewier than could be
Fizzing up tastily in my mouth.

I can smell
Beautiful red roses in a pretty pot
Cheese and tomato pizza cooking in the old dirty oven.

Jessica Paul (8)
Buckingham Primary School, Buckingham

It's A Wonderful World

I can see
A huge black Minotaur stomping around
A dark wood of dead trees.

I can hear
Brown murky water tumbling off
A huge, black, rocky waterfall.

I can smell
Horrible brown dirt from the
Damp floor,
I can also smell Minotaur poo.

I can taste
Nice red strawberries and I can also taste
Brown chocolate cake.

I can touch
Lovely smooth black rock and I can also touch
Silky wood.

Nathan Crisp (8)
Buckingham Primary School, Buckingham

In The Wonderful World

In the wonderful world
I taste mouth-watering unbearable sugar.

I see quiet cute mice
And my beautiful mum.

I hear
Crunchy feet stepping
And some lovely birds tweeting.

I can smell
Delicious food
And a smoky BBQ.

I can touch
My silky fluffy dog.
And a clean smooth marble.

James MacAleese (8)
Buckingham Primary School, Buckingham

What Do Storms Do?

What do storms do?
Crash and bang and splash,
Wake everyone up in the house,
Shoot fireballs of hail pattering on the roof
Like clattering bells

What do storms do?
Make rivers and lakes wild like
Animals in the same cage,
Make rocks crash down the hill like
Cannonballs setting off

What do storms do?
Bang, crash, there go our tiles
On our roof,
Another tax to pay,
Dad will be doing that all day!
What will be the storm's next victim?

What do storms do?
Blow leaves to and fro
Up and down but they don't keep them low,
Then they throw them down and start something else

What do storms do?
The plants are growing happily,
But they're going to sleep just for a while,
That while becomes soon,
The storm whisks them up like
A big metal hand grabbing onto them

Who do storms pick?
Unfortunately we are the storm's next victim!
So hold on tight and say hello to the night,
For that's when the storm will strike.

Alice Choulerton (9)
Buckingham Primary School, Buckingham

Millie In The Storm

Lightning crashed
Thunder roared
She's not scared, she's not scared

Rain boomed like fireworks
Wind whistled like a jolly postman
She's not scared, she's not scared

Then something tapped her on the shoulder
She turned around, nothing was there
She's scared, she's scared

The hail was still patting
The river had overflowed
But Millie was inside safe and sound.

Ella Louise Circuit (8)
Buckingham Primary School, Buckingham

During The Bad Weather

During the bad weather I heard
Wolves howling like thunder rumbling

During the bad weather I saw
Lightning striking and flashing fiercely

During the bad weather I felt
The hail like a herd of
Elephants charging over me

During the bad weather
The wind whirled like
10,000 tornadoes.

Hannah Weatherley (9)
Buckingham Primary School, Buckingham

During The Storm

During the storm
I saw the rain
Crashing down
Like a rampaging rhino

During the storm
I heard thunder
Booming down
Like an elephant
Stomping

During the storm
I saw lightning
Lighting up the
Beautiful
Midnight sky

During the storm
I heard hail
Falling out of the sky like
One thousand
Golf balls

After the storm
I saw beams of
Light coming through
The gaps in
The treetops.

Charlotte Vernon-Stroud (8)
Buckingham Primary School, Buckingham

During The Storm

During the storm
The wind whirled like a
Pack of wolves eating their prey

During the storm
Rain crashed like two
Cymbals clashing together

During the storm
Thunder roared like
A lion roaring to protect family

During the storm
Lightning was a firework
Flickering in the inky black sky

During the storm
Hail bounced up like
Bits of fire flicking in the moonlight

The river was wild
Killing every fish instantly

The clouds had cleared
The storm had passed.

Zak Momen (9)
Buckingham Primary School, Buckingham

What A Wonderful World

I can see,
Horses galloping around with their
Shiny coats glistening in the sunlight,
Flowers blooming happily together.

I can hear,
Minds working with ideas buzzing around,
Crisps crunching while bumping
Around in their mouths.

I can taste
Creamy chocolate melting like icicles,
Squeegee sweets being squashed
By their teeth and bursting.

I can smell
Brown, crispy bread heating up in the cooker,
Luscious bacon sizzling in the pan.

I can touch
The smooth yellow petals of a flower,
The smooth, silky, white feathers of a bird.

Eloise Gibson (8)
Buckingham Primary School, Buckingham

The Wonderful World

I can see
The hot gleaming sun shining brightly on the flower-fresh flowers.
Waves clasping gently to shore.

I can hear
The graceful softness of birds flying and singing, tweeting a morning song.
Fresh cut grass floating in through my window.

I can taste
The melting caramel
Chocolate in my mouth.
The sweetness and sticky pink floss in my mouth.

I can smell
The sweetness of the freshly baked bacon.

Chloe Talbot (8)
Buckingham Primary School, Buckingham

During The Storm

During the storm
The wind whistled like a policeman
Walking in the street

During the storm
The thunder roared like a hungry lion

During the storm
The lightning flashed like a TV screen

During the storm
It hailed like mad

During the storm
The hail made holes in my raincoat
And the lightning made me blind
The thunder made me cry
And the wind blew my pants off.

Joe Cooke (8)
Buckingham Primary School, Buckingham

During The Storm

During the storm
The wind whirled like a hurricane
Ripping tiles off a roof
During the storm
The wind whistled like a referee blowing
His clean, loud whistle

During the storm
Lightning flashed like fireworks
Exploding in the night sky
During the storm
Lightning flashed like smoke balls firing.

Joseph Clancy (8)
Buckingham Primary School, Buckingham

During The Bad Storm

During the storm,
The wind whistled like a pack of howling wolves

During the storm,
The lightning flashed really badly right in
My dark brown eyes

During the storm,
The raindrops dropped one by one

During the storm
The thunder roared like a lion
Frantically in a zoo.

Stuart Rudd (8)
Buckingham Primary School, Buckingham

It Was So Quiet That . . .

(Inspired by 'A Poem to be Spoken Silently' by Pie Corbett)

It was so quiet
That I could
Hear my heart
Beating slowly.

It was so quiet
That I could
Hear a small
Dog barking
In the distance.

It was so quiet
That I could
Hear a butterfly's
Wings beat.

Luke Jones (8)
Buckingham Primary School, Buckingham

If I Were A Bird

If I were a bird
I would touch the fluffy clouds
That drifted in the gentle soft air.

If I were a bird
I would swoop in the air
Near the blazing hot sun.

If I were a bird
I would collect the pretty
Bare brown sticks
That lay on the park.

Grace Gregory (9)
Crowthorne CE Primary School, Crowthorne

Sheep

Sheep are fluffy,
As white as snow,
They mow the lawn,
By eating so.

Grazing in the meadows,
The green grass meadows,
They chomp and chew on a juicy snack.

Enjoying the sun,
The blazing sun,
They sunbathe in their favourite spot.

Having some fun,
Lots and lots of fun,
They spring around the meadows having their morning run.

Ella Zwarteveen (9)
Crowthorne CE Primary School, Crowthorne

Black Dot

A black dot
A jelly dot
A punting puffer
A belly flopper
A slimy body
An eye stayed put
A staring thing
A tongue so long

A black dot
A diamond dot
A wet pebble
A leap frog
A round spot
An inky blob
A button to press
A counter to flick

A black dot
A looking pupil
A midnight moon
A dirty coin
A hairy mole
A lump of coal
A speck of dirt
A full stop.

A black dot
A pinch of skin
A grain of pepper
A sunflower seed
A furry mark
A stag beetle
A chirpy blackbird
What a black dot means to me.

Mia Reeve (7)
Crowthorne CE Primary School, Crowthorne

Paintbrush

If I were a paintbrush
I would smell the scent
Of wet paint
As sweet as a blooming rose.

If I were a paintbrush
I would hear the clouds
Whispering quietly to the sun.

If I were a paintbrush
I would look into people's
Hearts and paint a happy picture.

Lia Butterworth (9)
Crowthorne CE Primary School, Crowthorne

Three Months

October, Octobre,
Schools are out
Halloween comes,
More trick and treating,
And sweets, too.

November, Novembre,
Back to school,
More work to be done,
Bonfires burning,
Fireworks going bang!

December, Décembre,
Holidays come again,
Sleigh bells ringing,
Happy faces,
Jesus' birthday.

Adam Bennett (7)
Crowthorne CE Primary School, Crowthorne

All About A Fish

I went for a snorkel
And got caught in some coral.

I saw lots of fish
Shooting past my eyes.

They were blowing bubbles
In my face.

Ruby Allerton (7)
Crowthorne CE Primary School, Crowthorne

Monkeys In The Zoo

In the zoo cute monkeys swing in the trees
In the zoo cheeky monkeys throw coconuts at me
In the zoo funny monkeys pull faces
In the zoo hungry monkeys eat from their food bases
In the zoo monkeys eat bananas and nuts all day long
In the zoo some monkeys are very strong
In the zoo all the monkeys look like they're in a trance
Then they break into a dance.

Hannah Tomlin (7)
Crowthorne CE Primary School, Crowthorne

Aeroplane

Aeroplane, aeroplane in the sky,
Is it black or is it white?
Aeroplane, aeroplane in the sky,
It's so hard to say goodbye.
Aeroplane, aeroplane in the sky,
Can you see me when you pass by?
Aeroplane, aeroplane in the sky,
I can't find you anywhere.
I looked in the airport, I looked in the sky,
Where are you? I'm going to cry.

Bader Alhout (10)
Hillside Primary School, Lower Earley

Crystal The Husky

Her eyes are blue
Like the sky above.
She always gives me lots of love,
She is black and white and fluffy,
Her name is Crystal,
A Siberian Husky.

Will Agate (11)
Hillside Primary School, Lower Earley

Chester

Chester, Chester Copperpot is his name
And he's my dog
With floppy ears and sparkly eyes
Like a star glittering in the sky.

He has a spotty belly
That wobbles like a jelly
And snores so loudly he shakes my house.

I love him and he loves me
Every time I cuddle him
It feels like a tree.

Doulton Fuller (11)
Hillside Primary School, Lower Earley

Rabbits

Rabbits eat carrots, and scare parrots
Rabbits like to hop! Hop! Hop!
Rabbit sleeping in its cave, having a crave
Rabbits like to hop! Hop! Hop!
Rabbits like to play with you, as long as you don't have your shoes
Rabbits like to hop! Hop! Hop!
Rabbits should be out of the cage, or they will have a strong rage!
Rabbits like to hop! Hop! Hop!
Rabbits don't show affection, but be sure to pay attention
Rabbits like to hop! Hop! Hop!

Sirui Wang (10)
Hillside Primary School, Lower Earley

Rainbow

Rainbow, rainbow
Lovely rainbow.
You are up,
Up in the sky.

Different, different
Colours above.
They add beauty,
To the sky.

Rainbow, rainbow
Lovely rainbow.
You never end,
In the sky.

Rainbow, rainbow
Lovely rainbow.
You are up,
In the sky.

Natalie Olembo (10)
Hillside Primary School, Lower Earley

The Beach

Sitting on the seaside in the great big sun,
Licking on an ice cream and eating a great big sausage bun!

Children using their suncream,
As the sun is shining on them like a massive beam.

A lonely child making a sandcastle,
While the other children are playing a beach game of pass the parcel.

The kids have a great old moan,
Because the mum says, 'It's time to go home!'

Jack Bingham (10)
Hillside Primary School, Lower Earley

Dogs

Some dogs are cute,
Some dogs are fluffy,
Most dogs have tails, and really long nails.

Some dogs are brown,
Some dogs are black,
Some dogs are golden and really fat,
Some dogs are thin,
Some dogs are small.

Some dogs have short legs,
And some are really tall.

My dog is all of those except golden, fat and tall,
I love my dog because she is so cool!

Sophie House (11)
Hillside Primary School, Lower Earley

Dreams

Dreams can be good
Dreams can be bad,
Dreams can make you happy,
Dreams can make you sad.

I much prefer the happy ones
That make me smile and gleam.
I want to dream
That I'm eating lots of ice cream.

But dreams are what you make them,
And you have them every night,
Sometimes you wake up excited
And sometimes you wake up with a fright.

Kayleigh Winship (10)
Hillside Primary School, Lower Earley

PJs

PJs can be soft
PJs can be rough
PJs can have monkeys on or cats or giraffes
PJs can be pink
PJs can be blue
PJs can be checked
PJs can be short
PJs can be long
PJs can be quarter length
PJs can be tight
PJs can be trousers

But mine are purple, black and blue,

PJs can be spotty
PJs can be stripey
PJs can have cows on
PJs can have sheep on
PJs can be purple
PJs can be white
PJs can be baggy
PJs can be stretchy
PJs can be smooth

But what I have described is what all mine are like!

Rebecca Maplethorpe (10)
Hillside Primary School, Lower Earley

The Sunshine

I woke up in the morning,
The warm sunshine shone on my whole body.

I looked out of the window;
The warm colours made me feel excited to get up.

The warm colours made me feel like it was another fresh day.

I looked out the window and I saw the seagulls making their cries
Flying around in the hot sun.

Harveen Mann (10)
Hillside Primary School, Lower Earley

Tropical Rainforest

Tropical rainforest, there's so much you can see,
Elephants, giraffes and baby chimpanzees.
So many creatures all around,
Up, down, even on the ground.

All different sizes,
Big and small,
Short and fat,
Skinny and tall.

Some are blue
Some are white,
Some who are friendly
And some who bite.

Tropical rainforest
I love it all,
They're all so friendly
They're all so small.

They're all so colourful
So beautiful and bright
Half are dark,
Half are light.

Aysha Ali (10)
Hillside Primary School, Lower Earley

Haunted House

I crept towards the window
Looked around inside
Something tapped me on the back
And gave me such a fright
I looked around behind me
Nothing could I see,
Not even my hand right in front of me!

Georgia Townsend (11)
Hillside Primary School, Lower Earley

Christmas Is Coming

Out of the box,
Once a year,
Means Christmas time
Is nearly here.

Open its branches,
Tall and straight
It's Christmas time
I cannot wait.

Dressing the tree with tinsel,
Then decorate it with balls,
Everyone is helping
Fun is had by all.

Turn on the lights,
The colours are bright,
Our Christmas tree lights up the night.

On Christmas Eve,
When we are all asleep,
Santa comes,
A silent creep.

All excited we cannot sleep,
Our presents wrapped
We want to peep.

We wait until the night is done,
Happy Christmas
Everyone!

Elizabeth Evans (10)
Hillside Primary School, Lower Earley

The Terror House

Welcome to the Terror House,
Where danger awaits!
Spiders, roaches and other creepies,
That you all hate.
The moon is full and bright,
And you will see what can't be seen
On any other night.
I know you're in for a real fright.
As soon as you take a step inside,
Prepare yourselves and hold your breath!
'Cause this may lead you to your death.
But as I'm your friend
I won't take you there.
Although you may go alone
If you *dare!*

Sohaib Ansari (10)
Hillside Primary School, Lower Earley

Darkness

Darkness rules the night,
Fighting off the light.
Wearing a black crown,
Making people frown.
If you go in the dark tonight,
Please turn on the light.
Before it rains,
And darkness rules again.

Jeremy Twala (10)
Hillside Primary School, Lower Earley

Halloween

Let's have a party now it's Halloween,
Invite my friends round, I'm so keen.
We'll all dress up and try to freak
The people living in our street.

I'll need my coat, bag, a torch too,
We'll have some fun that's what to do.
Have a dinner, toads and nails,
Fingers, slugs and slimy snails.

A spider cake with ghost meringues
Let's be Dracula with giant fangs;
I'll bite my victims one by one -
One hundred of them all in my tum.

Pumpkin lanterns glow all around,
Ghostly laughter's a scary sound.
The sky is dark, the moon is bright,
Ready for ghouls to come tonight.

We go to bed and listen hard,
Our ears alert, our eyes on guard,
Every noise gives us a fright
On spooky, scary Halloween night.

Pippa Way (10)
Hillside Primary School, Lower Earley

School Just School

At school it could be fun!
At school it could be boring!
You never quite know until you go!
Here's a thing when you get into year 6
You have to be neat and tidy
And get up early in the morning without moaning or groaning!
In class you look at the teacher with your arms crossed
And on the playground you walk around like you're the boss!
As you laugh and shout and run about!
School is just school, just be yourself, listen and learn because
School's just school!

India Holder (11)
Hillside Primary School, Lower Earley

My Cats

Al and Jude,
Are my two cats
Al is long and skinny
Jude is short and fat.

They sleep all day
And play at night
Al likes the bath
And Jude likes to fight.

Jude will go hunting
Catching birds, frogs and mice
Leaving us gifts
Which aren't very nice.

Al is getting old now
And just wants to rest
Unless he sees the tuna tin
Cos he likes that the best!

Harry Card (11)
Hillside Primary School, Lower Earley

Eid

Eid is a special day,
When kids can all play,
Friends and family get together,
Depending on the weather,
There's lots of yummy good food to eat,
Including samosas, kebabs and dishes of meat,
Lots of presents are exchanged,
If you don't like it, you can get it changed,
It is a jolly good time of fun,
But soon it ends and it's time to run!

Mohammed Khan (10)
Hillside Primary School, Lower Earley

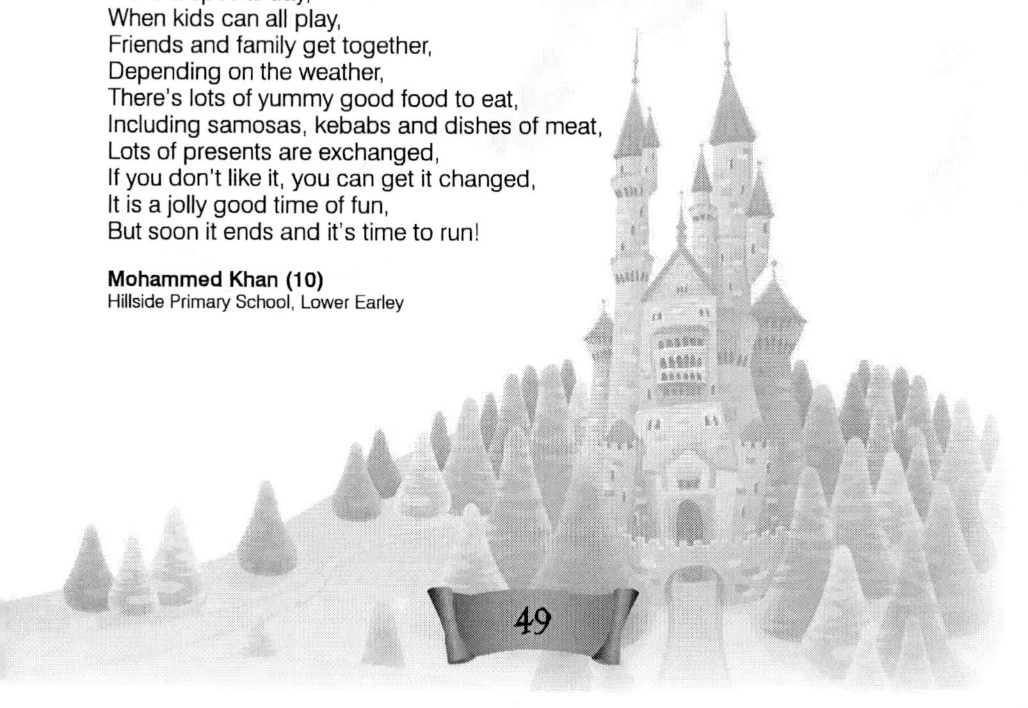

Space Travel

I love looking into the darkness of space
It puts a smile on my face,
I wonder what happens
In the furthest stars,
And if there is life on the planet called Mars?
Jupiter is shooting asteroids away from us,
Keeping us safe on the planet Earth,
I do one day wish to visit Saturn's rings,
How much fun will that bring?

Georgie Dunham (10)
Hillside Primary School, Lower Earley

Chocolate

I love chocolate rather a lot,
I will eat all I've got,
I like it on my cakes,
Especially the ones my mum bakes,
Give me a Mars bar any day,
And I will give you some Milk Tray,
My favourite of all is a bag of chocolate Revels,
When I eat them I turn into a devil!

Ciera Thompson (11)
Hillside Primary School, Lower Earley

Goblins Poem

Big ones, small ones, sort of in-between ones,
Hairy ones, slimy ones, scaly ones and fluffy ones,
Goblins! Goblins!
Fat ones, skinny ones, square-shaped ones and circle ones,
Rude ones, kind ones, shouting ones and quiet ones.
Goblins! Goblins!
Scary ones, cute ones, buck tooth ones, and no teeth ones
Goblins, goblins, *argh!*

Joshua West (10)
Hillside Primary School, Lower Earley

Rocket

Oh rocket, rocket way up high
Oh rocket, rocket in the sky
Where will you go?
Where will you land?

Oh rocket, rocket way up high
Oh rocket, rocket in the sky
Will you go far?
Will you go fast?

Oh rocket, rocket way up high
Oh rocket, rocket in the sky
What will you pass?
What will you see?

The Earth, the sun
The moon or stars
Probably Pluto
Maybe Mars.

Jordan Cook (10)
Hillside Primary School, Lower Earley

Spring

Spring is where the birds sing,
You could even find a fairy ring,
But you couldn't put it on a key ring.

It is also where the eggs are hatching,
Where the chicks are emerging
And the cats are purring.

The horses are running in the fields playing,
The cows are mooing
And the flowers are growing.

It is also where the rivers are flowing
The fireflies are glowing
Where the wind is blowing without knowing.

The frogs are bouncing,
It is where the sailors are rowing
And the noise of the children just keeps on going!

Isobel O'Connor (10)
Hillside Primary School, Lower Earley

Winter

Winter is the cold time, when it starts to snow,
Children look outside their windows and watch the stars glow.
The lakes are freezing over, icicles are forming,
It's getting so cold the fires need warming!

People wrapping up to step outside into the chilly breeze,
Keeping warm is essential because if you're not you'll freeze.
Hats and gloves, coats and boots, you need the whole lot,
If you don't you will need to check what you have got!

Winter is full of surprises just for you,
The celebration most people enjoy is Christmas, don't you?
Winter brings the snow along, it looks like a beautiful white sheet,
Snow is extremely cold, no wonder there is no heat!

Winter is a season, an amazing wonderland,
It looks fantastic, you could describe it as grand.
So winter is the cold season and some don't jump and say whoopee
But if you think it is great then come and take a walk with me . . .

Naomi Powell (10)
Hillside Primary School, Lower Earley

Trojan Horse

In the courtyard of Troy, the Trojan horse stood gigantic and proud.
It stood motionless, like a chess piece waiting to be moved.
The silence inside the horse was eerie
If you listened carefully all you could hear was the synchronised breathing
Which made the horse seem to be alive.
The Spartan soldiers were poised, ready to pounce
Like a cheetah ready to kill his prey.
The Trojans were blissfully unaware of what was to come,
Sleeping like babies!
The setting of the flaming sun signalled the ruthless attack was about to be unleashed
Like a lion caged up as a coiled spring.
As darkness fell the Trojan horse's hidden doors flung open,
And the Spartans, like the ruthless lion, were set free.
The fall of Troy began!

Robert Bedingfeld (10)
Hillside Primary School, Lower Earley

Butterfly

Butterfly, butterfly fly away
Fly away for me,
Don't let them catch you,
If you want to be free.

If you want everyone to see,
All your beautiful colours
On your fluttering wings
Then off you go, fly away
If you want to be free.

Butterfly, butterfly fly away
Fly away for me
I don't want to catch you
I want you to be free.

I want everyone to see
All your beautiful colours
On your fluttering wings
So off you go, fly away
I want you to be free.

Paige Jones (11)
Hillside Primary School, Lower Earley

Autumn

Autumn is windy and breezy,
Brightly coloured leaves swirl down from the trees,
Orange, yellow, red and brown
Landing softly on the ground.
As people walk the leaves are crunching and in the cold
Their shoulders are hunching.
The wind in the trees makes the sound of whistling,
The animals collecting acorns are bristling.
As the sun sets on this cold autumn day
It's time to go home in the warm where hot chocolate is waiting.
Family together and board games to play.

Zoe Cox (10)
Hillside Primary School, Lower Earley

My Brother Josh

Hates to have a wash,
He screams and shouts,
And runs about!

My brother Josh,
Has a sip of his squash,
He spills it on the floor,
Then he slams the door!

My brother Josh
Goes bish, bash, bosh,
When he runs down the stairs,
But he never cares.

Megan Priest (10)
Hillside Primary School, Lower Earley

Who Am I?

I am a comedian,
I have been in show business for over twenty years.
I have my own peanut range,
I have my own TV show on ITV1.
I can do impersonations of many different people,
I wear big-collared white shirts and huge glasses,
I have a bald head, which is always shiny.
I make humour of other TV shows, to attract my own audience,
I have also done my own roadshow at the Hexagon,
A sell-out performance for all different age groups.
I am the narrator for the TV show 'You've Been Framed'
Have you guessed it yet?
Who am I?

A: Harry Hill.

Vikram Brar (10)
Hillside Primary School, Lower Earley

The Forest

The forest is a wonder
Which is like a mystery
With no one there to reveal it
It will take its place in history.

The forest is a disco
Prancing all around
With the flowers boasting
It's quite an annoying sound

The forest is a wizard
Changing all the leaves
But there is one problem
What will he do with his two long sleeves?

The forest is a party
It's Christmas now
Bells, singing all around
How did I miss that? Oh how?

Alexandra Isaacs (8)
Hillside Primary School, Lower Earley

Little Seeds

Little seeds we sow in spring
Growing while the robins sing,
Give us carrots, peas and beans,
Tomatoes, pumpkin, squash and greens.

And we pick them
One and all,
Through the summer
Through the fall
Winter comes then spring
And then little seeds we sow again.

Qaynat Ditta (10)
Hillside Primary School, Lower Earley

My Football Final

The clock struck two
When the whistle blew
Like the rest of my team
I thought this must be a dream
We knew we had to win this game
Not just for the fame
To win the cup was what we wanted to achieve
We knew we could do it and could really believe
The game just flowed
And our skills showed
The ball was kicked to me
And then it hit my knee
It bounced on the floor
I knew I had to score
I kept my head low
I knew where the ball should go
My heart was thumping
As the goalie started jumping
But it was bad luck for him
As I kicked the ball straight in
I had just scored
And the crowd just roared
We had actually won
And now our work was done
The team were filled with pride
With the trophy by our side.

Tom Baskerville (10)
Hillside Primary School, Lower Earley

Liem

My name is Liem and I like to fight
My mum takes me boxing on a Tuesday night.
I wear black bandages and big red gloves,
I have to train hard to get real tough.
When I am older I want to become a pro,
Become rich and make lots of dough,
Because I'm small I will be a featherweight,
I'll work real hard and never be late!

Liem Sharp (10)
Hillside Primary School, Lower Earley

My Little Friend

I dream I have a little fuzzy friend
Its eyes are as shiny as the moon
It's fluffy and cute, it's like a penguin
But it's as loud as an elephant
As small as a mouse
It jumps like a frog
Swims like a fish
It flies like a kingfisher

But it was just a dream,
But a lovely dream!

Olivia Rowell (7)
Hillside Primary School, Lower Earley

My Worst Nightmare In The World

I was tucked up in bed
Ready for sleep
But then I woke up again!
A strange creature came up to me,
With knobbly knees,
And smelly feet.
I licked one of its toes
And it wasn't so sweet.
With a face like a hedgehog's back.
With ears as sharp as a crocodile's teeth.
With a voice like three gorillas shouting.
Then I woke up,
It was time for school!

Bhanusha Kirupakaran (7)
Hillside Primary School, Lower Earley

When The Sky Is Blue

When the sky is blue
I can see clearly too
My mum is there
She's sweet, I like her like that
Can't I be like that?
When the sky is grey
It's because I don't get to play.
I feel sad when it's like that.

Anishka Nair (7)
Hillside Primary School, Lower Earley

Steve Eats Anything

Steve eats
Anything
Leftover sandwiches
Ham and mustard
Last night's curry
Covered in fungus
When he's walking
When he's sitting
On a stool
Or on a wheelchair
On the bus
Or in the park
In the light
Or in the dark
Mouldy cheese
And squashy mushy peas
What he eats
Will make you howl
His eating habits
Are really foul
Steve eats
Anything.

Jasdeep Dhingra (9)
Homefield Preparatory School, Sutton

One Thing I'll Never Be

I'll never be a nought,
A zero, what you call it
I might be quite short
But not a nought.

I might be a cook
Or even write a book
But I am so intelligent
I could become the president
Or a seller in a shop.

But I'll never be a nought
Maybe work in a court
But being a nought is nothing.

I could be a rapper
Or a dressed-up kidnapper,
So much to choose from.

But the one thing I'll never be, is a nought.

Samuel Smith (9)
Homefield Preparatory School, Sutton

Nought

Don't be a nought,
Just give it a thought,
Being a nought won't help,
It hasn't got a personality,
Or even a dream.
No one is a nought,
In space,
Or even on the beach.
If you try your hardest,
Let your thoughts flow,
You'll never be a nought,
No, never, no, no.

Aston Barringer (9)
Homefield Preparatory School, Sutton

Life

Life is not fair
You might get strife
You will be what you will be
But you can be anything,
An astronaut, a scientist,
Maybe even Brad Pitt.
You can be it, you can be it
Just try.
If you set your standards high,
You could even fly.
But you have to try,
So please try
You can be it, you can be it
If you set your standards high.

Huw Shopland (10)
Homefield Preparatory School, Sutton

One Thing I'll Never Be Is A Nought

There's one thing I'll never be, that's a nought.
I will always be someone.

I might not be the king of pop
Or the best comedian.

This is where the crying stops
Now come out of that black, dark corner now
Come out, *get a life . . .*

Right, you may not be the best
At least you've got something

Use that to your advantage
Become a star
If you can't do it, try it.

But don't, don't
I repeat, don't fake it
You'll regret it
I promise.

Tiarnan Craine (9)
Homefield Preparatory School, Sutton

Sweet Smelling Tissue

So much depends on a tissue . . .

Embellished with a natural smell
Nestling in a sparkling tissue box.

Luke Saitch (9)
Homefield Preparatory School, Sutton

One Thing I'll Never Be Is A Blank Page

Maybe I'll be an engineer.
Or a man in the bar getting drunk on beer.
Or maybe a vet.
Or stay at university and be teacher's pet.
Or maybe a shadow who stays at home.
And can't afford shaving foam.
Or maybe a dad and have my very own lad.
But I'll never be a blank page.

Oscar Pitkethly (9)
Homefield Preparatory School, Sutton

One Thing I'll Never Be Is A Nought

I'm not a nought
A port or even
Very short.
Zero, none, same as nought
Station, bus stop, same as port
Tiny, little, same as short
One thing I'll never be is a
Nought, port or very short.

Leo Lim (10)
Homefield Preparatory School, Sutton

Autumn

A utumn is so boring like everything
U nder the trees where leaves fall,
under the trees where the conkers fall
T rees are good because they give us paper
U nder the trees where the fruit falls in autumn, the figs fall
M aybe it's hot, maybe it's cold, I don't know so don't ask me
N ever forget the day the holiday starts.

Matthew Scott (8)
Homefield Preparatory School, Sutton

The Thingy

Squishy, yucky, squishy as goo
Yuckier than you!
I call him Thingy.
Thingy loves to eat gloves and meat!
My thingy is called Thingy the Great.
I love my thingy.

Thomas Mercieca (8)
Homefield Preparatory School, Sutton

Winter

W inter is coming
I t's almost here
N ow's the time to store food
T oo bad, it's almost here
'E veryone dress warmly'
R ight, now it's here!

William Gurney (8)
Homefield Preparatory School, Sutton

Homefield

We are in the best school,
We all rule and others drool,
We are winning all the time,
Doesn't cost us a silvery dime.

Everyone's got a talent in a different way,
Some are smarter than others but others like to play,
Hooray, hooray, hooray, hooray, hooray,
Hooray, hooray, hooray, hooray, hooray for Homefield.

Colton Freigang (9)
Homefield Preparatory School, Sutton

The World

W ide is the world
O ver the mountains
R ivers and seas
L ong are the roads and
D angerous are the cliffs.

Sam Martin (8)
Homefield Preparatory School, Sutton

Leopards - Cinquain

Sleek, slim
Gleaming climber
Vicious bite to kill prey
Fast running cat, poor stamina
Waiting.

Imran Shaikh (9)
Homefield Preparatory School, Sutton

Pets

I hate pets, they're not nice
They eat everything
Even my lovely rice
When they behave bad it always rings a bell
So I will never buy a pet
Ever again.

Aditya Yanamandra (9)
Homefield Preparatory School, Sutton

Tigers - Cinquain

Tigers
Sneaky, agile
So cute yet so vicious
Striped skin that makes 'them' the parched ground
Waiting.

Alex Sun (9)
Homefield Preparatory School, Sutton

A Soft Dog

A little soft dog came up to me,
I took it home as it had a bad cough!
He was ill as he ate out of a trough.

He learnt to climb a wobbly ladder
And climbed all the way up to the loft.

Max Bowen-West (9)
Homefield Preparatory School, Sutton

The Cat

The cat walks out of his bed noisily
His fur black as the night
But his stomach white as the moon
His nail sharp as a knife
His skin pink as a pink rose
His eyes green as grass.

Louis Vasili (9)
Homefield Preparatory School, Sutton

My Pet Meerkat

My pet meerkat is called Mumble,
Because he tumbles down a hill at top speed,
But when he gets down to the bottom of the hill,
He gets into a very big jumble,
And thinks he's in the deep, deep jungle.

It's funny when I watch him play all day,
Because he thinks he's a big bad tiger,
And when it gets too dark in the day I have to tell him not to play,
For he must come home with me, have his tea, do his homework,
And watch the TV.

Goodnight dear Mumble, happy dreams to you and me.

Harry Andre (9)
Homefield Preparatory School, Sutton

Sport

S is for swimming, kicking your legs, throwing your arms
P is for polo-riding on a horse, hitting the ball
O is for oh yes I have won!
R is for respect and sportsmanship
T is for tears of happiness.

Sam Heape (8)
Homefield Preparatory School, Sutton

The Lonely Tiger

Back-scratching tiger,
Walking down the street.
Was born in Niger,
Hoping for some animals to meet.
He roared and he caught,
Lovely little deer.
Then he thought
Is anyone here?

Vivek Desai (9)
Homefield Preparatory School, Sutton

My Pet Monkey

My pet monkey is a very funky monkey
He is a little chunky monkey
And has no six pack
But he doesn't like to be locked up in a sack.
He doesn't like the bright light
But does like the holiday sight.
He is very hairy
But does not believe in a fairy.
He is very silly
But he calls everyone Billy.
My monkey is the best
He never likes to have a rest.
My pet monkey is the best monkey ever.

Yasser Malik (9)
Homefield Preparatory School, Sutton

Autumn

A time where leaves fall off
U sually see really tall trees
T here are trees tall and high
U sually you see really wet days
M ight see some sunny days
N uts falling off.

Anthony Marden (8)
Homefield Preparatory School, Sutton

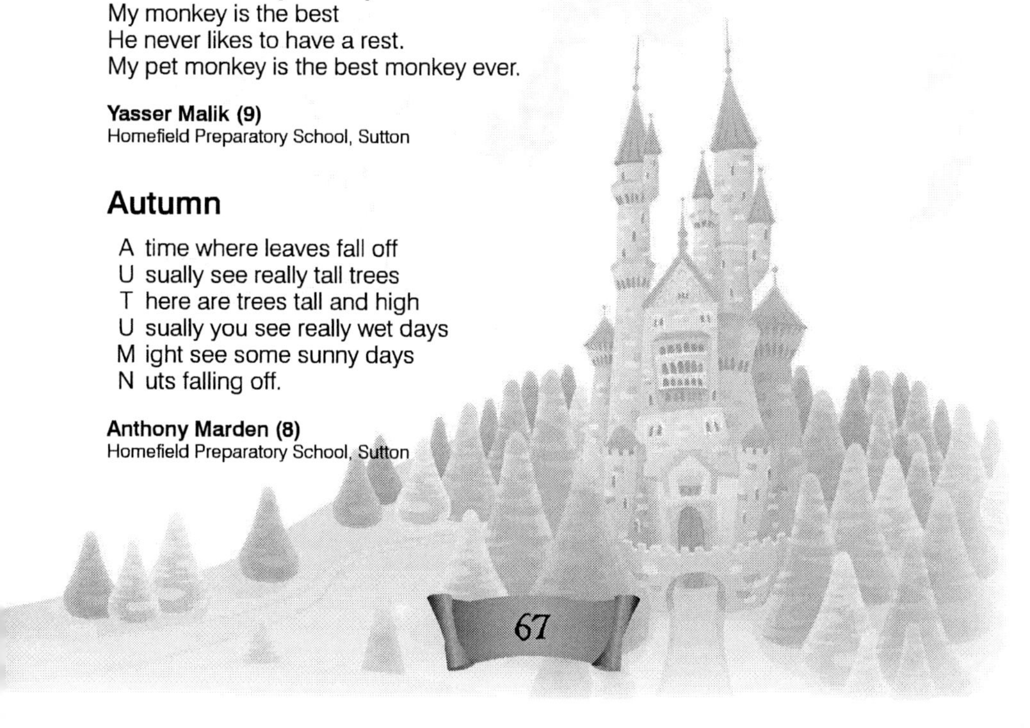

What Shall I Do Today?

I went to ride a train
Or fly a plane to Dubai
I could go and book my flight
The only thing I'm afraid of is heights
I could go to the train station and buy honey
The only thing I don't have is money.

Nasir Zahir (8)
Homefield Preparatory School, Sutton

Aeroplane

A eroplanes flying through the sky
E very day I would fly
R oaring engines
O ver the sea
P ast the mountains
L ashing through the air
A n aeroplane I wish to fly
N ot a car, not a boat
E asily my choice is to fly an aeroplane.

Alexander Morgan Davies (8)
Homefield Preparatory School, Sutton

Winter

W inter is great.
I n winter you will say it is great.
N ever, ever run away from winter.
T imothy says, 'Never run away from winter because winter is fun.'
E ach winter you will like it and love it, that is why winter is fun
because everyone likes it.
R un away from winter, Timothy will get you!

Faraz Chitalya (8)
Homefield Preparatory School, Sutton

Be Cool

If you go to school, you'll be cool.
If you don't you'll be a fool.
You won't be able to afford to go to Dubai's pools
So decide if you wanna be a fool or cool or see a pool
You could be washing dishes or making wishes
So set your standards high.
Be cool.

Nickan Panjehshahi (8)
Homefield Preparatory School, Sutton

There Once Was A Schoolboy Named Jack!

There once was a schoolboy named Jack,
Who carried his world on his back,
People who wondered why
Thought his locker was too high
But really he just liked his sack.

Jack Barone (8)
Homefield Preparatory School, Sutton

Volcano - Haikus

The volcano fired
The lava exploded out
Everything dried out

The icy cave shook
Shook like a big volcano
And the ice shards fell.

Arun Subramaniam (8)
Homefield Preparatory School, Sutton

Water - Haiku

Water is so blue
Waves in water, waves, waves, waves
Brilliant to swim.

Daniel Cronje (8)
Homefield Preparatory School, Sutton

The London Statue

I drove to London in my car
Then saw a statue with a jar
We suddenly stopped
When we saw it had hopped
For it should have been stuck down with tar!

Peter Neilan (8)
Homefield Preparatory School, Sutton

I Like Chocolate - Haiku

I like chocolate
Because it melts in my mouth
And it tastes so good.

Keir Dawson (8)
Homefield Preparatory School, Sutton

Winter Robin

Winter robin perched on the bough
Warming up her eggs
A head went *pop!* out came one
Then another, then another
Each giving mother a great fright.

Tom Reed (8)
Homefield Preparatory School, Sutton

Beautiful Nature - Haiku

No one's seen this wood
But I, this very moment
From this big oak tree.

Tom Bradshaw (8)
Homefield Preparatory School, Sutton

Shiv

Shiv is my name
I live down the lane
I go to Homefield School
Which is really cool
I have some mates
That lick their plates
Especially when it's pasta
They lick it even faster.

Shiv Rana (8)
Homefield Preparatory School, Sutton

Cheetahs - Haiku

Cheetahs speeding fast
Faster than the speed of light
Always catching prey.

Noah Yamin (8)
Homefield Preparatory School, Sutton

Monkey Yum - Haiku

Monkey eating gum
Sitting in the tree, yum-yum
Yum-yum, scrummy-dum.

Samuel Warren (9)
Homefield Preparatory School, Sutton

Life Is What You Live

Life is what you live
Life is everything you could wish for.

Being what you want or
Thinking what you are.

Makes no difference every day
So what I'm trying to say is,

Life is what you live,
Life is everything you could wish for,
Make your life important to you
And use your life wisely.

So don't waste it all,
It doesn't matter if you're big or small.

Giles Winterbourne (9)
Homefield Preparatory School, Sutton

You Can Make It

You can make it
You can take it
You can see it
You can be it.

The story is in your hands
The story could maybe stand.

Never, never, never,
Don't endeavour.

Fahd Khan (9)
Homefield Preparatory School, Sutton

Steve Eats Anything

Steve eats
Anything
Leftover sandwiches
Ham and mustard
Last night's curry
Covered in custard
When he's walking
When he's sitting
On a loo
Or on a cow
On the bus
Or in the park
At the mall
Or when he calls
In the light
Or in a fight
Mouldy cheese
And squashy fleas
What he eats
Will make you howl his
Eating is really foul.
Steve eats anything.

Caleb Bond (9)
Homefield Preparatory School, Sutton

Dead Fred

There was an old man named Fred
Who liked to stay in his bed
But one day the bed broke
And it make him choke
He tumbled to the floor and was dead.

Joe Howat (8)
Homefield Preparatory School, Sutton

Dustbin

So much depends upon . . .
A dustbin
Embellished with dirt
Nestling in the garage.

Rohan Rahman (9)
Homefield Preparatory School, Sutton

The Hanky Of Importance

So much depends on a
Hanky of importance.
Embellished with green emeralds all around it.
Nestling in the diminutive packet inside the greyish pocket.
How can you live without it?

Shrey Sachdeva (9)
Homefield Preparatory School, Sutton

There Once Was A Man With A Hat

There once was a man with a hat
Who thought he was humongously fat
But in fact he was thin
With thick crocodile skin
And a grin like a big Cheshire cat.

Harry Messent (8)
Homefield Preparatory School, Sutton

A Doctor Or A Surgeon?

If you want to be something, try your best
Be an architect, be a nurse or a doctor
You can be anything if you try hard enough
Don't be a nobody
Get your standards high and try your best at
English, maths and science
Be the best at your life test.

Oliver James Hemsley (9)
Homefield Preparatory School, Sutton

Seaside

When I am at the seaside I like swimming
And collecting those crunchy shiny sparkly shells
When I am at the seaside I like going in the sea
Because of the fresh salty seaside water.
The fish like it too
Because they wriggle and tiggle
They serve and sway about in the water.
The seaside ocean is very salty
Seaside and the grains of sand . . .
Crunch, crunch.

Caitlin Cartner (8)
Longcot & Fernham CE Primary School, Longcot

The Ocean

I like to dive in the sea.
To see orange clownfish lined with white stripes.
The waves are as rough as sanding paper.
To see sea urchins like cannonballs all spiky on the rocks.
And last but not least on coral reefs
Anemones like jelly wobbling on the plate.

I like to go wave watching
But I would really like to find the key to the Atlantic gate!

Alfie Togher (7)
Longcot & Fernham CE Primary School, Longcot

Fishing

I like fishing in the big blue sea
It gives a lot of fish for me.
Bait on the hooks catches the trout
Now it always comes clean out.
Sharks and tuna eat the cod
Sometimes they will escape from my fishing rod.
Whales and nets catch the pike
They're the fish we really like.
Crab lines catch the crab
Watch out their claws grab.
Flounder disguise themselves on the seabed
They keep still and pretend they are dead.
This big blue sea is the place for me.

Lewis Swinford (8)
Longcot & Fernham CE Primary School, Longcot

A Trip To The Sea

I like to fish in the sea
It has lots of fish for me
There are crabs and lobsters
Prawns and shrimps
Mackerel and cod
All dishes for me

As I go further into the sea
It has more fish for me
There are catfish and dogfish
And pollock and pike
That's my trip to the sea
I hope you like it like me.

Rory Smith (9)
Longcot & Fernham CE Primary School, Longcot

The Lake

The lake is as calm as the wind on a calm day
The fish hide away from a big bad heron
Shiver in their scales from fin to head
The running water glitters in the shimmering sun
The water is calm until
A man in the shadows casts his rod
Look out fish, this isn't fun.

The bait is rotten
That is good
The water shakes
Then the man shouts 'A bite!
Here's my bite for my tea.'

When fishing for my tea
I go to the lake
The lakeside is quiet
There's no one about
Except for me and the trout.

Beatrice Mercer (8)
Longcot & Fernham CE Primary School, Longcot

Ocean

The ocean is as blue as a highlighter pen
Some fish are as green as my mum's new top
Sardines are as silver as the moon
Sometimes the ocean is like an orange
When the ocean is rough.

Rosie Brader (8)
Longcot & Fernham CE Primary School, Longcot

The Floods

Oh my, oh my
A flood I hear you cry
People are drowned
People are on the ground
In the flood.

People do not have food
They do not have water
People are getting killed
Houses are losing build
In the flood.

There is no medicine for when you're ill
People are about to kill
People are losing their houses
Even little mouses
In the flood.

There are germs in the dirty water
Swimming to and fro
People are screaming and running
I know, I know, I know
In the flood.

There's whooshing and pushing
Splashing and wheezing
In the flood.

Mabel Leighton (7)
Longcot & Fernham CE Primary School, Longcot

Sea

Fish, fish, goodness me
All the fish in the sea
Salmon and mackerel, catfish too
Cannot survive without water
Like me and like you
Sparkly waters, foamy edges
Waves bashing against rocky ledges
Fish deep in the sea,
Seaweed wobbles like jellyfish
The sea can be rough
It can be smooth and be tough
So when at sea
Think carefully like me.

Zakk Carver (8)
Longcot & Fernham CE Primary School, Longcot

Me And My Mates With Our Roller Skates

I play with my mates,
On my roller skates,
We do funky spins,
Around the bins,
We do cool jumps,
But we end with bumps,
Me and my mates with our roller skates!

We go up ramps,
With our lamps,
We show off our funky wheels,
When our mum calls us in for meals,
We say goodbye,
We end on a high,
Me and my mates with our roller skates!

David Jones (8)
St Mary's Catholic Primary School, Churchdown

I Have A Dream

I have a dream that the lovely world will stay beautiful and every person be sharing.

I have a dream that the steel blue oceans stay the same and lots of fish stay alive.

I have a dream that the aqua blue sky stays healthy and stays up in the sky.

I have a dream that the happy children go to a caring school and learn something.

I have a dream that the tiny babies grow happily and sensibly.

I have a dream that all the cheerful adults be careful taking care of the children and their own self.

Muskan Mehra
St Mary's CE Primary School, Slough

I Have A Dream . . .

I have a dream that the busy world is as good as gold.

I have a dream that the steel-blue oceans are nice and clean
for all the scaly fish.

I have a dream that the azure skies above are very breezy
and refreshing for the feathery birds.

I have a dream that the playful children are always working extremely hard
and co-operatively with one another.

I have a dream that the cute babies are kept safe.

I have a dream that all the clever adults will not get annoyed
by the children not listening to them.

Anya Carroll (8)
St Mary's CE Primary School, Slough

I Have A Dream . . .

I have a dream that the great world is as sweet as a sugar candy cane.
I have a dream that the aqua-blue oceans glimmer more.
I have a dream that the beautiful sky has more sunshine.
I have a dream that the joyful children can learn more.
I have a dream that the cute babies grow well.
I have a dream that all the strict and angry adults will be more kind and loving.

Atharv Desai (9)
St Mary's CE Primary School, Slough

I Have A Dream

I have a dream that the azure world is so shiny and round.
I have a dream that the everlasting oceans are so bright aqua-blue.
I have a dream that the beautiful skies above are so slate-blue.
I have a dream that the cute children are so joyful.
I have a dream that happy babies will always be happy.
I have a dream that all the cheerful adults will stay cheerful.

Vickram Cheema (9)
St Mary's CE Primary School, Slough

Untitled

I have a dream that all of the countries are equal in the world and it is fair as well.
I have a dream that all the oceans are peaceful and unstormy.
I have a dream that the blue skies above are safe for the birds.
I have a dream that the 'over the moon' children are cheerful.
I have a dream that the merry adults are safe and children are safe as well.

Kamran Khan (9)
St Mary's CE Primary School, Slough

I Have A Dream

I have a dream that the oceans are clean to drink.

I have a dream the aqua skies above are going to stay the same.

I have a dream that the desperate children are cared for.

I have a dream that cute babies are getting comfort every second of every minute.

I have a dream that adults will treat kids how they should be treated.

Tywanné Patrick (8)
St Mary's CE Primary School, Slough

I Have A Dream

I have a dream that the vast world is as sweet as a sugar lollipop!

I have a dream that the aqua-blue oceans are as cold as ice!

I have a dream that the gigantic skies above are always going to stay warm and humid!

I have a dream that the confident children are always going to stay brave!

I have a dream that tiny babies are always going to grow up to be what they want to be!

I have a dream that the jolly adults will always be kind!

Faizah Saleem (9)
St Mary's CE Primary School, Slough

I Have A Dream

I have a dream that the beautiful world is as sweet as a sugar candy cane.

I have a dream that the amazing oceans are filled with beautiful living fish.

I have a dream that the wonderful blue skies above are filled with different types of beautiful birds.

I have a dream that lovely children are smart and helpful.

I have a dream that newborn babies are cute and adorable.

I have a dream that all the kind adults care for children.

Annabeth Gyamfi
St Mary's CE Primary School, Slough

I Have A Dream . . .

I have a dream that the beautiful world is as sweet as a sugar candy cane.
I have a dream that the fish in the oceans are nice and cosy.
I have a dream that the blue skies above are sunny and happy.
I have a dream that the naughty children are turned into good children.
I have a dream that small babies are going to be good adults.
I have a dream that all the adults are going to help each other.

Rumman Mujahid (8)
St Mary's CE Primary School, Slough

I Have A Dream

I have a dream that the lovely world is as sweet as a sugar candy cane.
I have a dream that the beautiful oceans are filled with lovely fish.
I have a dream that the lovely skies are blue above our beautiful countries.
I have a dream that the lovely children stay safe.
I have a dream that the kind babies are safe too.
I have a dream that the adults appreciate me.

Hamza Shahid (9)
St Mary's CE Primary School, Slough

I Have A Dream . . .

I have a dream that the beautiful world is as sweet as a sugar candy cane.
I have a dream that the colourful oceans are never the same every day.
I have a dream the cloudy skies above us are floating gently across.
I have a dream that the joyful children never tell anyone they're the boss.
I have a dream that all the cute babies always have fun.
I have a dream that all the bossy adults learn some sums.

Aisha Mohamed (8)
St Mary's CE Primary School, Slough

I Have A Dream

I have a dream that there is no killing for fun
Everyone will unite as one,
I hope that there will be peace
And all the crimes will cease,
And that is my dream.

I have a dream that everyone will say grace
And everyone will have a smile on their face,
I hope that we will be in a community
That there'll be lots of opportunities,
And that is my dream.

I have a dream that each person will be loved
By God and Jesus from above,
I hope that we will be loved the same
And reach our certain aim
And that is my dream.

I have a dream that people will respect themselves and others
Love each other like sisters and brothers,
I hope that hunger will end and that peace will begin
And that it wouldn't matter about the colour of our skin,
That is my dream.

Eliot Jones
St Mary's CE Primary School, Slough

I Dream . . .

I dream to be someone useful,
And to be wise.
I dream to be successful,
And to be kind.

I dream to be happy,
And to be healthy.
I dream to be famous,
And to be wealthy.

I dream of a nice house,
And to have a good job.
I dream of a long life,
And never want to sob.

Abby Melvin (9)
St Mary's CE Primary School, Slough

I Have A Hope

I have a hope, a hope to fulfil my dreams,
To make me lots of ice creams!
My dreams have all come true, what about you?
I love ice creams,
So sweet and tasty,
I love ice creams,
Like homemade pastry
I wonder how you make soap - I have a hope.

I have a hope, a fantasy,
To help me through reality,
My favourite ice cream is choc chip,
It looks just like lipstick,
I love ice cream,
So sweet and tasty,
I love ice cream,
I wonder how you make soap - I have a hope.

I have a hope, a hope to fulfil my dreams,
To make me lots of ice cream!
My dreams have all come true, what about you?
I love ice cream,
So sweet and tasty,
I love ice cream,
Like homemade pastry
I wonder how you make soap - I have a hope.
I wonder how you make soap - I have a hope.

Fizza Waheed
St Mary's CE Primary School, Slough

I Have A Dream

I have a dream that there will be no more war and fighting.

I have a dream that they will follow the law.

I am worried about Year 6 and in secondary school.
I will feel nervous when we are ready to do the exams.
I will feel very nervous.

I want to start a new life by doing as I am told.
I want my future to be bright by working hard.

Danyal Imran
St Mary's CE Primary School, Slough

My Dream

I dream of floating away on a cloud,
I dream of catching a falling star,
I dream of my Prince Charming,
I dream of how I'll save him from the dragon,
I dream of cats talking at night,
And a giant bowl of milk running for freedom.

I dream of old ladies knitting socks,
I dream that twelve elves are real,
I dream I'll meet them someday,
I dream of monkeys swinging me about,
I dream of a bed of roses,
And how prickly that must be.

I dream of a chocolate field,
I dream of me being famous,
I dream of being tall,
And I dream of being short.

Now I stop here,
Going back to my dreams,
I will be back tomorrow,
With more.

Sweet dreams.

Ekambir Sahota (9)
St Mary's CE Primary School, Slough

My Dream

My dream is that all the wars stop,
And all the countries be friends,
My dream is that everyone stops killing animals,
My dream is that all the poor people stop being poor,
My dream is that people stop cutting trees down,
My dream is that people care for trees and grow them,
My dream is that everybody is happy in life.

Shannon Hidri (10)
St Mary's CE Primary School, Slough

I Have A Dream

Another name, another body, another sacrifice;
I have a dream that war will end,
That no other child will lose a parent
In the face of war.

I have a dream that countries will stand together
To put their differences aside;
To help those who have suffered through war
And help them to a future.

I have a dream that the children of my age
Will make this happen
Because we have the belief
That peace is better than war.

The children of this world,
Will hold hands and work together,
So that my dream, will be
All children will shout, 'Let's end this war!'

James Hammond (9)
St Mary's CE Primary School, Slough

I Have A Dream

I have a dream to become a music teacher.
I hope I get into college some day.
I would like to be like my music teacher when I grow up.
Some day I would like the wind to blow in my face
And a letter landing in my hand saying that I am in college.

Some day, if I get into college, I would be able to go to university.
I have a dream to become this.
I have a dream to become a well-behaved student.

I will feel happy, I will be proud of myself and I will feel lucky.
I would like to become the luckiest person in the world,
I think the teachers would like my work.

Tabitha Burgess (9)
St Mary's CE Primary School, Slough

I Have A Dream!

I have a dream, for people rich and poor to get along in peace and harmony.
No fighting, no killing and no criminals, not at all.

I absolutely have a dream that concerns every sufferer in Lebanon, Pakistan,
China, Haiti, Palestine and many more.

I hope the world will unite one day and look into the war in Lebanon,
The invasion of Palestine and the disasters that occurred in Pakistan, China and
Haiti.

I have a dream that when I get older I will represent these unfortunate people
from that day on!
I would like to help these people in bad conditions for their safety and health,
And for people to know that they can do lots to help them.

I also have a wish that every vulnerable child or adult should hear and know that
we are there for them and that we are going to help them in their suffering!

Alaa Fawaz
St Mary's CE Primary School, Slough

I Have A Dream

I dream of catching a falling star
I dream of everyone getting along
World at peace no more wars
Everyone is happy.

I dream there are no more poor people,
No hungry children, no disasters at all.
I want everyone to be united
I dream everyone is positive.

I dream of everyone's dream to come true.
I dream of angels guiding me through.
I have to go now.

Have a lovely sweet dream.

Kian Cameron Kaur Dosanj (9)
St Mary's CE Primary School, Slough

My Hope

I hope I will be a . . .
I hope I will be a great footballer one day,
I hope I'll be the best and that's how it might stay.
It may be true you will never know,
So come people, let's go and play,
Play, play.
Every day is a different way to show.

My dream is to . . .
My dream is to score for a famous team,
Reality might be inside my dream.
Today may be the start of the great team,
So come people, start practising
Practising, practising.
Let's get into my awesome dream.

I desire to be the . . .
I desire to be the best footballer in the world,
We will always play in the rain and cold.
Everyone would know my famous name,
So come people, get my autograph
Autograph, autograph.
All of this could be my *huge* aim!

Hatif Ahmadzadah (9)
St Mary's CE Primary School, Slough

I Have A Dream

I have a dream that one day all the people in the world will live together in harmony.
That they will love, co-operate and care about each other and not just money.
All the wars of the world and the killing will come to a stop.
I hope that peace, love and kindness will be at the top.

I have a dream that families will not fall apart.
That all the people will be of one heart.

I dream of one country, one nation, united by me.

I dream that the leader of that nation will be me.

Panashe Dzumbunu (9)
St Mary's CE Primary School, Slough

I Have A Dream

I have a dream that I could be a doctor
I have a dream that I had a Ferrari
I also have a dream that I could get no older
But most of all I have a dream that
There were no racist people and robbers
And the world can stick together and be friends forever.

Shameel Allymamod (9)
St Mary's CE Primary School, Slough

I Have A Dream!

I have a dream to be a teacher like Miss Collet.
Kind, helpful and very stylish.
Teaching everybody art is what I wish to do.
Helping the rude, good, and even the childish too.

I am longing to get my driving licence.
Being in my own car.
In a black Honda sports car is what I want!
Travelling everywhere close and far.

I am so happy when my mum cooks my dinner.
Rice pudding, chicken, pasta, just so yummy.
I want more, more, more please.
All squashed in my little tummy!

Raakhi Sharma (9)
St Mary's CE Primary School, Slough

Winning Run!

Cricketers I admire,
That is why it is my desire,
To be a cricketer when I am older is what I
Want to be.
Sports is my expertise,
I'm very good at it.
I learn step by step, bit by bit
'The winning run is mine'.

Sarmad Ali
St Mary's CE Primary School, Slough

I Have A Dream

Hi my name is Memoonah, I'm going to tell you about my poem! Here I go!

I have a dream of painting with a colour so bright.

I have a dream of watching John Cena and Batista fight.

I have a dream of telling my mum an awful big lie,

I have a dream of eating a yummy pie.

I have a dream I pass my SATs test,
My teacher tells me I'm the best.

I have a dream I find a treasure map.

I have a dream I find my orange cap.

I have a dream my name is Tess.

I have a dream I'm thinking less.

I have a dream I am small.

I have a dream I am tall.

Memoonah Murtaza (10)
St Mary's CE Primary School, Slough

The World I Want It To Be

Why can't we all get along and stop doing things wrong?
Why don't we like people's faces just because of their races?
These are questions I struggle to answer when people ask.

Kindness these people lack,
Why can't they follow a good track?
One day I hope it will all really work
With none of us causing any more suffering or hurt.

A part of this new world I want to be,
Where everyone feels as equal be they a he or she
When I am older I want to say
I was there when it changed to the world I want it to be.

Holly Woodhouse (9)
St Mary's CE Primary School, Slough

I Have A Dream

I have a dream
That there is no such thing as racism,
That we can all be treated equally,
That there are no such things as war, weapons or drugs.

I have a dream,
That people will be kinder to each other,
That the war never came,
That there are no more coming wars.

I have a dream,
That there is no bullying,
That there is no killing anywhere,
That there is no dying, unless of old age.

I have a dream,
That the world will be in peace,
That we can all live happily together without any violence.

Celina Deniz (10)
St Mary's CE Primary School, Slough

I Have A Dream

I have a dream that one day people will not fight against each other.

I have a dream that one day people will not smoke.

I have a dream that one day people will stop war.

I have a dream that one day people will not swear.

I have a dream that one day people will not hit people.

I have a dream that one day people will not throw litter on the ground.

I have a dream that one day people will not go on dirty stuff like Facebook and such much more . . .

I have a dream that one day people will not treat their things with disrespect.

Amad Sheikh
St Mary's CE Primary School, Slough

I Have A Dream

Some people, they can't dream.
That makes them really mad.
Some people, they can dream.
But they are not thankful enough.
That makes me feel really sad.
When you dream it is so beautiful.

My dream is to have world peace.
People are always having war.
Can't we live in peace?
A dream is really amazing, *wow!*
A dream is really peaceful.
Just like the sound of the ocean.
To me that's what it seems.

If you dream it won't kill anyone.
These rubbish things about wars.
War is a nightmare not a dream, OK?
People complain and have a fight.
Can't people have a little bit of light?
It does not matter which religion you are.
Or what race you are, we are one.

We are all humans, aren't we?
I like to think that peace is my dream.

Bolaji Adepeko (10)
St Mary's CE Primary School, Slough

I Have A Dream

I have a dream that the world becomes friends.

I have a dream that everyone has the same rights.

I have a dream that everyone stays in peace.

I have a dream that there is no war.

I have a dream that people stay the same.

Zain Ashraf
St Mary's CE Primary School, Slough

I Have A Dream

I dream that . . .
Everyone would trust each other.

I dream that . . .
There would be no fighting in the world.

I dream that . . .
Everyone would get along.

I dream that . . .
No one would feel left out.

I dream that . . .
Peace would spread round the world.

I dream that . . .
Bullying would stop.

I dream that . . .
No one would waste anything.

I dream that . . .

Sadia Nawaz
St Mary's CE Primary School, Slough

I Have A Dream

I have a dream
That we can live in a world without any racism.
I have a dream
That there will be no more war.

I have a dream that,
There is no more bullying.
I have a dream that we can all live in peace.
I have a dream that we can be friends and one day hold hands.

I hope one day my dream will come true
And bring peace around the world.

Keannah Shaw (10)
St Mary's CE Primary School, Slough

I Have A Dream!

I have a dream that,
We all shall be one,
No one will be judged by their colour,
There will be no discriminating remarks.
We will stand by each other's side like brothers and sisters.

I have a dream that,
There will be no poverty,
Everyone will have food on their plate,
Everyone will have a roof over their heads and no one will be jobless,
Every child will have a school to go to.

I have a dream that,
There should be no slavery,
That people should be granted justice,
People should have freedom from every nation, every city, every valley
And have the freedom of right, have freedom of speech,
Have freedom from war.

I have a dream that,
One day there will be a ring of freedom,
Where we shall all sit together, eat together, pray together,
Be one nation with no injustice and no one will be helpless.

Zaynah Mughal
St Mary's CE Primary School, Slough

I Have A Dream!

I have a dream that the world would live in peace,
Like a lush ruby rose spreading its aroma in through angry people's noses And
making a big bright smile on top
Of their grumpy, upside down smiles.

I will dream some more; the world would hold hands together
In beautiful sunny weather, no matter what culture or religion you are,
Even if you have a tail or a feather.

I dream that the less fortunate people will have food to their fill,
And not face an enormous bill!
Not to suffer from starvation and children to have a good education.

I live in hope that one day, *magically,* my dreams will come . . . true!

Haleema Arfan
St Mary's CE Primary School, Slough

I Have A Dream . . .

I have a dream that there will be no war.

I have a dream that everyone will accept the law.

I have a dream that everyone will care.

I have a dream that together we can share.

I have a dream that the smiles will spread across the Nile,
And that love will travel miles and miles.

I have a dream . . .
I wish it would come true . . .

Ambreen Usman (10)
St Mary's CE Primary School, Slough

I Have A Dream

I have a dream there are no alcoholics
I have a dream for peace and quiet

I have a dream that all religions get along
I have a dream there's no war

I have a dream no one smokes
I have a dream that no one gets left out

I have a dream that the worlds will never end
I have a dream that everyone has a friend.

Karan Dholiwar
St Mary's CE Primary School, Slough

I Have A Dream

I have a dream that people will not pollute Earth

I have a dream that people will not do drugs

I have a dream that people will not kill or hurt others

I have a dream that people will have the same dream as me

So don't be afraid to dream.

Mazhar Islam (10)
St Mary's CE Primary School, Slough

I Have A Dream!

I have a dream that one day all the wars in the world will come to an end and there will be peace all over the world.
People from all different religions will be friends with each other and live in peace and harmony.
That there will be no cruel people in the world and we can trust everyone.
I have a dream that in every country there will be different coloured people so they can share all their different traditions.

I have a dream that everyone can have a chance to live a life free of poverty.
People will no longer live on the streets without any money or food.
That everyone is able to have access to a good education.
I have a dream that no one will be kept in captivity by other people and that everyone can be free from slavery.

I have a dream that we can live in a world without pollution.
People will act responsibly and take care of the environment around them.
That the homes of animals will not be destroyed due to many trees being cut down.
I have a dream that the natural environment will be preserved for many, many years to come.

I have a dream that one day the world that we live in *will* be a better place . . .

I have a dream!

Megan Ballard (10)
St Mary's CE Primary School, Slough

I Have A Dream!

I have a dream that everyone is treated fairly
I have a dream that no one is left out
I have a dream everyone is treated with respect.
I have a dream that there is no racism in the world
I have a dream everyone respects each other's culture
I have a dream that we all live peacefully.

Noosheen Saleem (10)
St Mary's CE Primary School, Slough

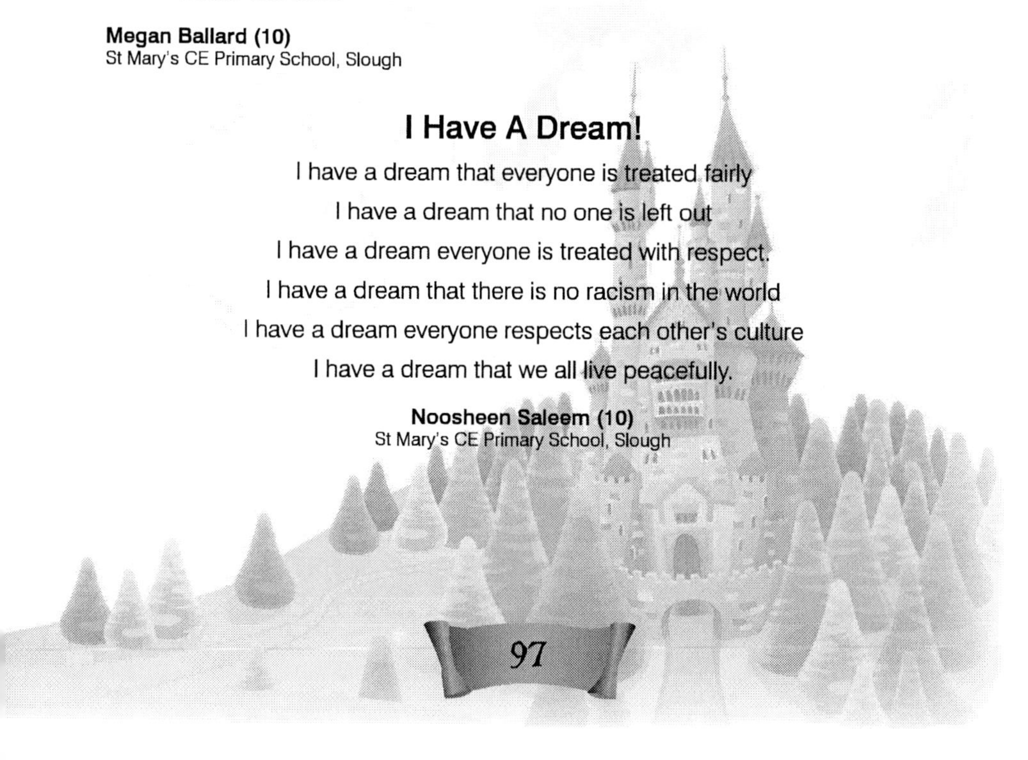

My Rap

My name is Hannah
But they call me Han
I've got a dog called Deefa
And a cat called Sam
I've got a brother called Daniel
He's just finished school
He's going to uni
Which is really cool
I've been to Ireland
Which was really wet
I took my neighbour
And my pet
I spend a lot of time
With my mum
We like to cook
And have some fun
I like to go out
With my dad
I buy new fish
Which makes me glad
My sister is Amy
We like to fight
We fight all day
We fight all night.

Hannah Germain (9)
Trevelyan School, Windsor

My Conker Bob

My conker Bob
Is as hard as a brick wall.
My conker Bob is as bold and shiny
As Anelka's head.
My conker Bob sounds like a clock
Ticking and rotating.
My conker Bob
Smells like rotten wood.

Vincent Widera (9)
Trevelyan School, Windsor

My Rap

My name is Amy
Hear me call,
I do gymnastics
Watch me tumble and fall,
When I do football,
I'm always on the ball,
Don't let me run
Into that wall,
Prefects tell me
'Don't run in the hall,'
Ellen is my sister
Who is quite tall,
My dad always likes
To watch football,
But mum is the very best
Of them all.

Amy Donaldson (9)
Trevelyan School, Windsor

My Conker

My conker is called Bruce
My conker is big
My conker is strong

Like a wrestler
My conker seems strong
My conker is as hard as a brick
My conker has the scent of fresh grass
My conker feels hard and sticky
Brown like some wood
As loud as someone knocking on the door
My conker is like a boulder
My conker is scary, awesome and mean
As brave as a giant under attack.

Bilal Ibrahim (9)
Trevelyan School, Windsor

A Rap About Me!

Yo my name is George,
I go to Trevelyan School,
I love football
Which is really cool.
I play in a team
Every weekend
We win a lot of games,
We don't have to pretend.
We will play a tournament
On the Isle of Wight.
It's on a weekend,
So we'll stay overnight.

I also climbed Snowdon
With my family.
The weather was so bad,
We could hardly see.
We made it to the top
In three and a half hours,
It was a real struggle
In the clouds and showers.
We were all soaked through
As we got to the top.
My mum went to the gift shop
And bought new socks.
The climb down was easier,
It took less time.
I really enjoyed it
And I hope you liked this rhyme.

George Cliff (9)
Trevelyan School, Windsor

My Rap

My name is Areya,
I go to Trevelyan School,
I've won lots of trophies,
Which is really cool,
I have a little brother,
Who is very lazy,
I have a big brother,
Who is also crazy,
I want a pet dog,
Named Scruffy,
Ballroom dancing
Which I like,
And sometimes
I like going
On my bike.

Areya Torjaroen (9)
Trevelyan School, Windsor

Chloe's Rap

Hi everyone
My name's Chloe
I've got a sister
Who's called Naomi
Ruby my rabbit
Lives in a hutch
She's grey and white
Because she's Dutch
My favourite subject
At school is art
Which has always been
Right from the start.

Chloe Adand (9)
Trevelyan School, Windsor

Autumn Poem

Autumn is a time
When leaves turn different colours
Such as brown, red, orange and yellow.
The grass, plants, trees and flowers become damp colours.
The leaves slip off the trees with a crash!
It becomes darker and colder.
All the acorns, pine cones, conkers and oaks
Lots of squirrels are about
To gather acorns, winter hibernation.

It's Bonfire Night
And Halloween
The wind is like you're sleeping in an ice bed.
The Bonfire Night fireworks is my favourite bit
I would say autumn is a wind-blower
Autumn is the season between the sunny summer and windy winter.

Abeer Mohammad (9)
Trevelyan School, Windsor

My Conker Poem

My conker is called Minddy.
She looks like a glistening goldmine from the depths of the deepest mines from centuries ago.

She is as frantic as a cheetah in the heart of the golden sun.

She is as deadly as a hippopotamus from under the depths
of the speeding river.

My conker is as strong as an eagle approaching its prey.

My conker is as brave as a god directing his lords.

Eve Haswell (9)
Trevelyan School, Windsor

My Conker Fatman

My conker is called Fatman
Because his sides are fat and bold
My conker shines like a glass
When the sun shines on it.

My conker smells of dirt when
It falls on the ground.
My conker rolls like a golf ball
When it drops on the ground.

Fatman my conker
Brave but fat
Weak as an ant.
My conker
Fatman.

Justyn Morris (9)
Trevelyan School, Windsor

My Conker Flash Bang

My conker is called Flash Bang
He's as fast as a flash and ends with a bang.
My conker is as smooth as frozen ice
And as shiny as sparkling water.
My conker smells like rotten wood
That comes out of a gutter.
My conker sounds like a bomb coming through the school roof.
Flash Bang is my conker.

Max May-McBride (9)
Trevelyan School, Windsor

My Rap

My name is Alex
I love ice cream
I like football
But I don't play in a team.
I have a sister
Daisy's her name,
Worm's Open Warfare
Is my favourite game.
My sister's friends
Annoy me a lot.
I've been to Japan
It was very hot.
I like my toys
Especially my RC car.
Once I went to Brighton,
It's surprisingly not far.
My favourite food is
Apple pie with custard.
I also like hot dogs with mustard.
My favourite subject is
Design technology
I have a friend
Called Mikey.
I have a lot of friends
But the best is James
I really like
Video games.

Alex Plumb (9)
Trevelyan School, Windsor

My Rap

Summer is here,
Shout, 'Yippee!'
Going to the beach
Splashing in the sea.
I go to see my nan and spend my money
We have lots to eat
Like toast and honey.
I like to play football
With my mates.
I play all day
It's getting late.
The day goes fast
And it's time for bed.
Up I climb
Then bang my head.

Alfie Martin (9)
Trevelyan School, Windsor

My Rap

My name is Abby,
My sister's Amy,
I like to bake,
A chocolate cake,
I like netball,
Which is really cool!
I went to Spain
On an aeroplane.

Abby Hattey (9)
Trevelyan School, Windsor

The Nonsense Poem

I saw a conker boot a ball.
I saw a firework sing in the hall.

I saw a tree hiss at a bee.
I felt the Earth go upside down.
I saw a pumpkin lantern talk to me.

I saw an orange drive an ox.
I saw an ox explode into seeds.
I saw a man spit out grapes.

I saw a paper grow four arms.
I saw a box breathe fire.
I saw a banana eat itself.

Chasraj Jhita (9)
Trevelyan School, Windsor

Autumn

Autumn is like the sunset of day, as the leaves glide from the trees!
There is Halloween, and children get greedy!
The squirrels start preparing for hibernation.

Soon it'll be winter, but my mum and brother's birthdays are first!
I think it's going to be a brilliant autumn!
There's time until Christmas,
But it's going to be wonderful!

Chloe Horne (9)
Trevelyan School, Windsor

Nonsense Poem

I saw SpongeBob suck up the sea.
I saw an elephant fight with a flea.
I saw a dog flip pancakes really fast.
I saw a ship with a snake as a mast.
I saw a hat having a dance.
Then I ran home while I had a chance!

Ben Elson (9)
Trevelyan School, Windsor

This Like That

The soft tiger in its den
Like a baby in its cradle
The angry wolf in its cave
Like boiling water in a pot.
The fuzzy tarantula in its tank
Like itchy wool in a shop window.
The huge pony in the toilet
Like a jack-in-the-box
The leopard cub in the grass
Like sunlight swimming through reeds.

Madeleine Tarrant (10)
Trevelyan School, Windsor

The Animal Poem

The roaring lion is in its cage
Like a criminal in its cell.

The tarantula is in its corner
Like a naughty kid at school.

The parrot on your shoulder
Like a toddler on a ladder.

The monkey swinging branch to branch
Like a child in the playground.

A cat in a basket
Like a baby in a blanket.

Lucy Macnab (11)
Trevelyan School, Windsor

The Night

The cold night is like a merciless black panther looking for its prey.
Stealthily moving between the shadows,
It is the ultimate hunter.

I pity those who fall victim to this cold-blooded killer.

Adam Wilkowski (10)
Trevelyan School, Windsor

The Sea Is A Wolf

The sea is a wolf
Growling and howling day and night
Running then pouncing on its prey
It is giant and grey
With its shaggy jaws
Licking its greasy paws.

And when the night wind roars and the moon rocks
In the stormy clouds
It howls and halloos long and loud.

But in November and December it is quiet and calm
The wolf is in its den on the muddy floor
Shivering, shivering, so cold.

Saira Khan (10)
Trevelyan School, Windsor

Animal Antics

The furry monkey swinging in the trees,
Like a wild toddler flying off her swing.
The soaring bird flying through the blue sky,
Like a kite bobbing around the clouds.
The fast, furious cheetah in the safari is,
Like a cat playing with its string.
The strong, enormous horses are in the stables,
Like the excited, colourful parrot in its cage.
The loud dog is in the garden,
Like a dolphin in the deep sea.

Dean Leavy (11)
Trevelyan School, Windsor

Similes And Metaphor

The snake in the long grass,
Like the pen in its case.

The dog in the park,
Like the pig in the sty.

The kangaroo in the safari,
Like the wild monkey in the jungle.

The flying parrot in the cage,
Like the haddock fish in the water.

The stripy lion in the circus,
Like the happy horse in the stable.

Natasha Chopra (10)
Trevelyan School, Windsor

Butterfly Dancer Poem

A butterfly is a dancer
Pretty and perfect
She flutters and flows everywhere she goes
With her pretty smile and glamorous clothes
Every second she moves and grooves
When she is in the mood
The butterfly dancer moans
In her lovely home.

Jade Lewis (11)
Trevelyan School, Windsor

My Animal Poem

Can you hear the sounds of windows smashing in the building?
Cars crashing on the road?
Wind blowing in the distance?
Grenades exploding in Afghanistan?
Dogs growling at the mailman?
Lions roaring in the zoo?
Guns shooting in the war zone?
Paper tearing over the bin?
Woodpeckers pecking in the tree?
Pianos playing in the opera?

Alfie Barnes (10)
Trevelyan School, Windsor

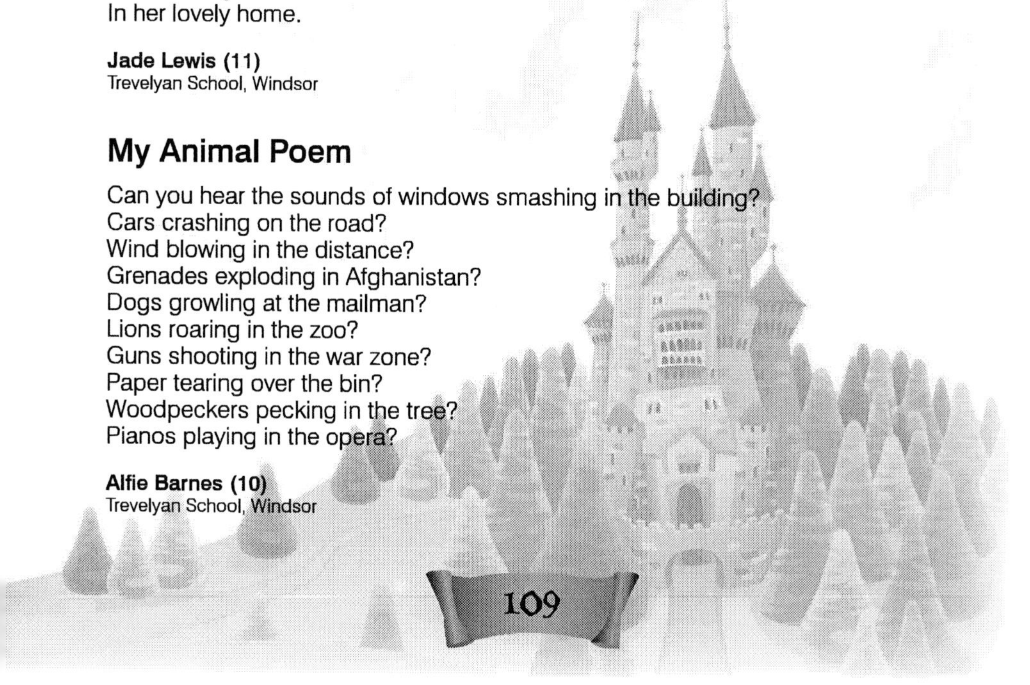

The Animal Poem

The fuzzy monkey high up in the treetop
Like a bird soaring the sky, looking for prey
The little brown kiwi in a bunch of leaves
Like a squirrel's nut pile underground
The small meerkat in its burrow
Like a person tucked up in bed
The green scaly crocodile in a river
Like an excited child in a pool
The black beetle in a piece of wood
Like a person in his house.

Charlie Pass (10)
Trevelyan School, Windsor

Metaphor Poem

The night comes like an assassin.
He comes like a flash of lightning.
Silently creeping up behind you.
He gets ready to murder any unlucky victim.
Stealthily passing his enemies.
He stays deep in the shadows.
Cunningly takes out his enemies.
He always plans how he will take out his next foe.
He is invisible to the people who try to kill him.
He travels by the light wind.
And can't be found by anyone.

Ryan Walker
Trevelyan School, Windsor

The Horse Of The Sea

The sea is a peaceful horse.
Foamy and white.
Peacefully galloping back and forth all day.

But don't be a fool, he can turn rough.
Splashing and tumbling.
On stormy nights he is very mad.
Throwing himself against the shore.

When he has calmed down he will let you ride him bareback.
Back to the safe shore.

Letitia Downes (10)
Trevelyan School, Windsor

Autumn

In autumn I see the trees blowing.
In autumn I can hear the wind screaming.
Sometimes I can see the trees reaching side to side.
When I am in my house I go into my bedroom
And wonder what autumn is like.

When I go outside I can see different pretty colours on leaves all up in a big group.
Then I jump into them.
Autumn is a lovely thing because I can smell lovely fresh shepherd's pie.
In the morning I can taste the lovely hot cocoa.

Sophie Cordice (9)
Trevelyan School, Windsor

Wind Poem

The wind blows and blows and moans and moans.
He lets his anger out on people and trees.
The people get blown and blown.
Also the trees get blow down.
The wind is a bully.

Jack Thomas Melton (10)
Trevelyan School, Windsor

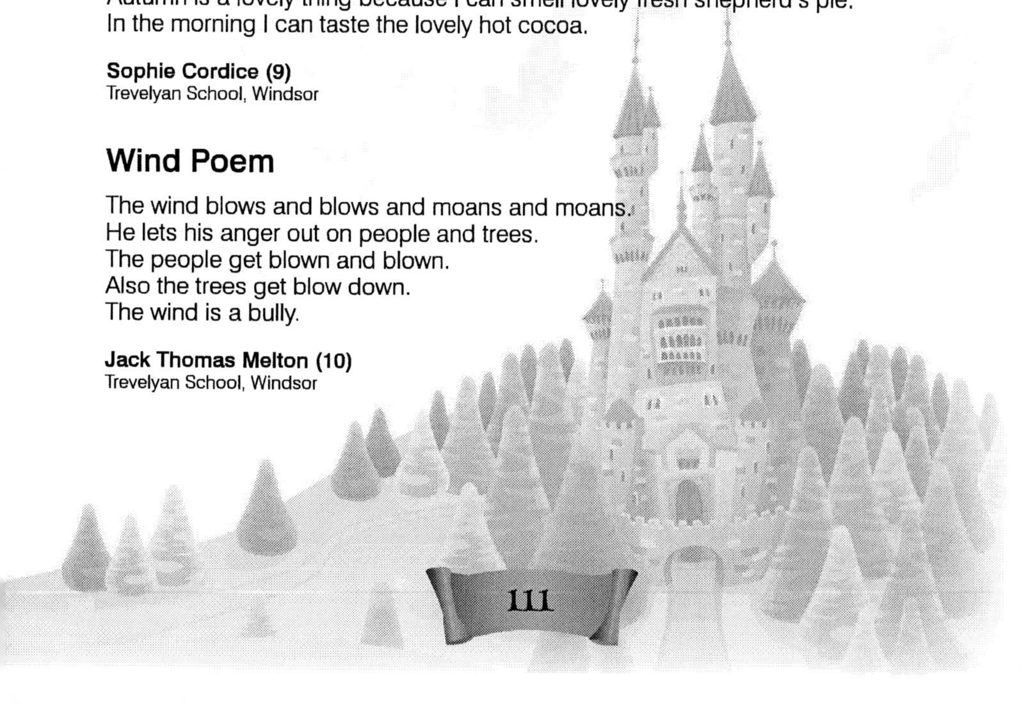

Autumn

The three months of autumn are my favourite time.
The leaves on the trees are as orange as the sun.
I love to crash through the leaves as they come tumbling down.
They make me smile from my head to the ground.

The wind whistles as it travels through the trees.
It yells like a child who has fallen to its knees.
The children play as autumn dies
And says goodbye to the orange skies.

Jack Greenwood (9)
Trevelyan School, Windsor

Autumn

Autumn, it's autumn, the leaves are brown.
The leaves are like tree trunks now
And the grey garden squirrels that go *boing! boing! boing!*

The earth has changed so much through winter, spring and summer.
My favourite part is collecting conkers
Crash as the leaves fling themselves as far as they can.

Fred Dearling (9)
Trevelyan School, Windsor

Autumn

Autumn is for fabulous fun
Trick or treat for everyone
Pumpkins glowing in the dark
Candles jumping around like a spark.

Bonfire Night is drawing near
When magical fireworks will appear
Pop and whizz the fireworks go
Then we look forward to the winter snow.

Ellie Lawrence (9)
Trevelyan School, Windsor

Autumn

Leaves whizzing round and round in the whistling wind,
Falling green from the trees, then red as a rose,
As orange as a pumpkin, yellow like the golden sun and then they turn crispy brown.
Clattering conkers crashing to the ground with their porcupine spikes,
Exploding out of their shells.

Flickering fireworks burst into the air, colours streaming everywhere,
Banging, whooshing and flashing like lightning!
Creepy cobwebs and skipping shadows,
Halloween is a spooky night,
Witches and ghosts give you a fright.
These are my memories of a freaky autumn night.

Hetty Brake (9)
Trevelyan School, Windsor

Autumn

Autumn leaves begin to fall
Trees now look very small.
The leaves crunch as people walk
The wind makes the trees talk.

As autumn sets in
The cold on my skin.
The trees look so bare
With no leaves to spare.

As night-time falls
The trees seem to call.
Birds are still singing,
My door is ringing.

My friends are here
As darkness is near.
It's Halloween tonight
Time for a fright!

Daniel Alinmore (10)
Trevelyan School, Windsor

Through The Woods

Crunch! Crunch! Crunch!
As I step on the leaves,
I walk through the woods to get to a conker tree
That grows conkers every autumn.
I pick some every year.

Plonk! Plonk! Plonk!
As the conkers hit the ground,
Patiently waiting in the grass to be found.
The green spiky shells of the brown shiny conkers
Prickle my fingers as I take one off.
Out pops the conker, as brown as chocolate.

Into my pocket it goes.

Evie Fawcett (9)
Trevelyan School, Windsor

Autumn

The wonderful leaves jumped off the tree.
Crunch! Pop! Bang!
Go the leaves when you step on them.

Crunch! Pop! Bang!

Ruby-red and bark-brown
The leaves lie like a crunchy rug.

Bang! Pop! Crunch!

Martha Pack (9)
Trevelyan School, Windsor

Autumn

In autumn the leaves fall on the grass.
They fall off the beautiful trees as I walk past.
When I look up to the shiny sun
I see the sun as orange as a pumpkin.

Two tall trees
Happy in the breeze.
The cheerful birds flutter their wings,
Not thinking what the weather brings.

Ivan Kwok (9)
Trevelyan School, Windsor

Autumn Is . . .

My sister's brilliant birthday,
Spooky Halloween,
Blazing bonfires,
Colourful leaves,
Hibernating hedgehogs,
Shiny, brown conkers,
Dazzling fireworks,
Plentiful harvest,
Foggy mornings and bare trees.

Maia Perkins (9)
Trevelyan School, Windsor

Autumn

As the door crept open the shimmering sun sparkled like a disco ball
Except for its natural
Drip! Drip! Drop!

As rain began to plummet down to Earth
A rainbow formed with the autumnal leaves of autumn falling to us.

Nina Smith (9)
Trevelyan School, Windsor

The Book That Never Ends

First an adventure, with princes, dragons and more;
A scaly, slimy beast with a dagger-like claw;
A damsel in distress in an ancient grey tower,
Wizards with spells and magical mystical power.

Next a love story, not much to say:
A beautiful young girl locked away,
A prince so kind, so charming and sweet,
To win her hand or be dragon meat!

Maybe a mystery, a crime on the street.
A brainy detective with a puzzle to complete.
A necklace missing, the gems just gone,
A robber swiping it as it glistened and shone.

How about some history? Back into the past,
Start at the beginning and discover first to last.
What about Egyptians with their pyramids so high
Not knowing that their structures would survive and never die?

What about a sequel? Does this book have one?
I don't know, but for now just keep reading on . . .

Jessica Tyler (10)
Winkfield St Mary's CE Primary School, Bracknell

The Book Fair

B efore you buy a book
O pen it and have a look
O therwise you might not . . .
K now what you have got

F or as long as I can remember
A book has always brought me joy
I love a good book better than a toy
R emember to visit the book fair
and always take care.

Alice Day (9)
Winkfield St Mary's CE Primary School, Bracknell

Halloween Poem

Ghosts scary as can be,
Spiders crawling all over me,
Bats flying in the dark,
Pumpkins glowing in the park,
These things happen on Halloween.

Witches cackling through the night
Ghost which give us a scary fright
Evil faces laughing out loud,
Spooky noises all around,
These things happen on Halloween.

Children going trick or treat,
All going home to eat their sweets,
Devils dancing all about
Everybody screams and shouts
These things happen on Halloween.

Ella Wallum (9)
Winkfield St Mary's CE Primary School, Bracknell

Little Red Riding Hood

As she crept through the night her cloak floated in the breeze,
A blood-red velvet cloak.
Then all of a sudden . . . *shh!*
She tossed and turned in the bed covers.
A pod of peas she found in her bedding
When she woke, seven others were gazing at her
Thinking of where she was heading.
Dumpy, Grumpy, Lumpy, Sumpy, Tumpy, Fumpy and Donald were their names.

The house was rather posh,
Round wooden chairs,
Fountains of water,
Statues of bears,
Paintings of kings and their daughters
Dashes of bright paint,
Baskets of dates.

'Apples my dear?' the frail woman asked.
Red grabbed an apple and took a bite.
All was quiet in the breezy night,
Ccrr-aackkk went the footsteps on a pile of some leaves.
I turned and looked but all I could see
Was a cloak floating in the breeze, blood-red velvet.

Lily Ellis (11)
Winkfield St Mary's CE Primary School, Bracknell

69 Days

Trapped
Closed in
Hot
Humid
Little food
Suffering
Want to get out!

Anxious
Squashed
Worried
Wobbly
Carefully
Winched
When is the end?

Bright
Wonderful
Relief
Happy
Jubilant
Hugs
Love
Fresh air
Miners.

Evangeline Bateman (10)
Winkfield St Mary's CE Primary School, Bracknell

What Is It?

I see a shape,
Wolf-like and grey,
I hear it howling,
Am I its prey?
Is it a hungry wolf ready to attack?
Am I tonight's dinner?
The light switches on,
Oh it's a dog.

I hear a sound,
A low, slow grumbling,
The stomach of a tiger ready to eat?
He must know his tummy's rumbling,
My hairs stand up,
And then I realise,
It's just me, I'm hungry.

I smell something horrible,
A vampire's breath?
Is he ready to devour my blood?
Oh, not long until death,
I'm ready to defend myself,
Then I realise,
It's my breath that smells.

I taste something bitter,
A curse in the air?
Will I be haunted forever?
Is the person who did this laughing in its evil lair?
I feel sick,
But then I work out,
It is the taste of sour juice.

I feel something sharp,
A pain in my head
Has someone got a dagger?
Will they press it in until I'm dead?
I want to think
Of some sort of conclusion but . . .

Jasmine Dhaliwal (10)
Winkfield St Mary's CE Primary School, Bracknell

Monkey Poem

Monkeys are cheeky
Monkeys like to play
Monkeys like to eat bananas
And go crazy all day

They go to a special school for animals
Where they learn how to swing on branches
Where they practise how to climb
Where they go cuckoo during lunches

Monkeys are hairy
Monkeys make a lot of noise
Monkeys are messy
Monkeys like to play with toys

I know them very well
I see them every day
They wear green cardigans
And they are my friends
Some may say.

Abbie Garrod (9)
Winkfield St Mary's CE Primary School, Bracknell

Autumn!

Conkers falling on the ground.
Leaves dropping from the trees.
It's getting colder.
Darker evenings.
Gold, brown and orange leaves.
Sitting by a roaring fire, toasting marshmallows
And sipping tea.
And best of all at the end of the year
We have Halloween!

Daisy Grimes (9)
Winkfield St Mary's CE Primary School, Bracknell

Book Song

When you open up a brand new book
Think about what you might read.
When you open up a brand new book
You will just want to read.

Pigs that can
Drive a van
A monkey who can talk
Fabulous things
Such as bears or kings
And maybe a witch or two.

A story or rhyme
Just take a look
And go and read a book.

Christopher Menon (9)
Winkfield St Mary's CE Primary School, Bracknell

A Day At The Beach

Sandy beach squirming through my hot toes.
Noisy oceans roaring like angry lions.
Eye-catching boats sailing into the pink horizon.
Multicoloured fish darting through the slimy seaweed.
Shallow rock pools filled with tiny creatures.
The scorching sun blazing onto the silver rocks.
The sunburnt crowds lying on their stripy towels.
Cool surfers riding the foaming waves.

Robyn Randall (9)
Winkfield St Mary's CE Primary School, Bracknell

Edward's Reading Rap

Mum says, 'Read!'
I say, 'No! The Simpsons are on, I've got to go.'

Dad says, 'Read!'
I say, 'Too late! The game on my DS is really great.'

My sister says, 'Read!'
I say, 'No way! My best friend wants to go and play.'

No telly, no games, I'll read my book.

The story is brilliant - take a look!

Edward Barnard (9)
Winkfield St Mary's CE Primary School, Bracknell

I'm Talking About . . .

Chatty mouths,
Big mouths,
Tiny mouths,
Gloomy mouths.

For kissing,
For talking,
For licking,
For laughing.

Look at those glossy mouths,
Look at those smiley mouths,
Look at those frowny mouths,
Look at those silly mouths.

Soraya Brooks (7)
Winkfield St Mary's CE Primary School, Bracknell

I'm Talking About . . .

I'm talking about bellies
Fat bellies
Skinny bellies
Rumbling bellies
Chunky bellies.

Bellies for belly-dancing
Bellies for eating
Bellies for hula-hooping
Bellies for the caterpillar.

Look at those yummy bellies
Look at those red bellies
Look at those juggling bellies
Look at those jelly bellies.

William Day (8)
Winkfield St Mary's CE Primary School, Bracknell

I'm Talking About . . .

I'm talking about teeth.
Loose teeth,
Chewing teeth,
Sharp teeth,
Clean teeth.

Teeth for grannies,
Teeth for chiefs,
Teeth for animals,
Teeth for thieves.

Look at those wobbly teeth,
Look at those bottom teeth,
Look at those biting teeth,
Look at those rotten teeth.

Sofia Gonzalez (7)
Winkfield St Mary's CE Primary School, Bracknell

I'm Talking About . . .

I'm talking about eyes,
Funny eyes,
Small eyes,
Sparkly eyes,
Tall eyes.

Eyes for jumping,
Eyes for blinking,
Eyes for looking,
Eyes for winking.

Look at those cat eyes
Look a those brown eyes
Look at those star eyes
Look at those blue eyes.

Now the eyes are closing to say goodnight.

Millie Turner (7)
Winkfield St Mary's CE Primary School, Bracknell

I'm Talking About . . .

I'm talking about hands
Clean hands
Mean hands
Old hands
Cold hands.

Hands for picking
Hands for hitting
Hands for sticking
Hands for knitting.

Look at those cool hands
Look at those bold hands
Look at those pool hands
Look at those boom hands.

Hands that say hello or
Hands that say goodbye.

Emily Adams (7)
Winkfield St Mary's CE Primary School, Bracknell

I'm Talking About . . .

I'm talking about ears
Big ears,
Floppy ears,
Tiny ears,
Spotty ears.

Ears for hearing,
Ears for clapping,
Ears for listening,
Ears for flapping.

Look at those furry ears,
Look at those foamy ears,
Look at those plain ears,
Look at those phoney ears.

Now these ears have to stop the excitement
And they will have to wait until the morning.

George Atkinson (8)
Winkfield St Mary's CE Primary School, Bracknell

Ruined Rhymes

'Mary, Mary, quite contrary
How does your garden grow?'
'With bugs and beasts and bits and twits
And weeds that you can mow.'

Jack and Jill went up the hill to fetch a
Pail of water,
When they came down they were married
Again and had a little daughter.

Twinkle, twinkle, little star,
How I wonder what you are.
Maybe a UFO or a plane
Little star you've gone again.

Tabitha Ludeman (8)
Winkfield St Mary's CE Primary School, Bracknell

Ruined Rhymes

Rock a bye baby on a cliff top
What are you doing up there?
Were you put there by Mummy
Sucking your dummy?
You're giving me rather a scare.

Three blind mice, three blind mice
Didn't know what to do
They really wanted some glasses
But the man at Specsavers said, 'Shoo!'

Twinkle, twinkle little star
How I wonder what you are.
Coming nearer and nearer,
Well I'm sure . . .
Wait a second, meteor . . . !

Oliver Breedon (9)
Winkfield St Mary's CE Primary School, Bracknell

Ruined Rhymes

Humpty-Dumpty sat on a wall
While his wife went to the mall
She came back with water, sugar and flour
And was in the kitchen for over an hour
Before Humpty-Dumpty knew his fate
He was a pancake
On a plate.

Isabelle Davis (8)
Winkfield St Mary's CE Primary School, Bracknell

Ruined Rhymes

Hey diddle diddle
The cat and fiddle
The moon jumped over the cow
The little mouse stopped to eat some cheese
And the dish and the spoon had a row.

Eleri Dadd (8)
Winkfield St Mary's CE Primary School, Bracknell

Ruined Rhymes

Three blind mice, three blind mice
See how they run, oh what fun.
They all bumped into the farmer's wife
Who chopped them up with her sharpest knife
And served them up with lots of rice
Three blind mice, oh how nice.

Flo Brockman (8)
Winkfield St Mary's CE Primary School, Bracknell

Ruined Rhymes

Hickory dickory dock,
The mouse ran up the clock,
Rather wished he'd not,
When he realised he had a watch,
By the time it got to nine,
The mouse had learnt to tell the time
And by the time it got to ten,
The mouse was back with Mum again.

Colleen Harcourt (8)
Winkfield St Mary's CE Primary School, Bracknell

Ruined Rhymes

Little Miss Muffet sat on her tuffet
Drinking a glass of Coke.
There came a fat monkey
Scratching his tummy,
She thought it was only a joke.

'Baa baa black sheep have you any wool?'
'No sir, no sir, no bags full
None for the milkman, none for the dame,
None for the annoying boy who lived down in Spain.'

Jack Hobbs (9)
Winkfield St Mary's CE Primary School, Bracknell

My Garden Poem

Daffodils, daisies and roses too
Are always covered in the morning dew.
Holly and heathers are very different
Because holly's got spikes and heather is as gentle as a feather.
Herbs, spices, peppermint too,
All go together to make a delicious stew.
Apple trees, orange trees, plum trees too,
I love fruit, do you?
This is my garden poem for you,
I hope you enjoy it too!

Eloise Shrewsbury (7)
Winkfield St Mary's CE Primary School, Bracknell

Young Writers Information

We hope you have enjoyed reading this book - and that you will continue to enjoy it in the coming years.

If you like reading and writing poetry drop us a line, or give us a call, and we'll send you a free information pack.

Alternatively, if you would like to order further copies of this book or any of our other titles, then please give us a call or log onto our website at www.youngwriters.co.uk.

Young Writers Information
Remus House
Coltsfoot Drive
Peterborough
PE2 9BF
Tel: (01733) 890066
Fax: (01733) 313524

Email: info@youngwriters.co.uk

Shakespeare Quiz Answers

1. Stratford-upon-Avon **2.** Romeo and Juliet **3.** James I **4.** 18 **5.** The Tempest **6.** Regan, Cordelia and Goneril **7.** His wife **8.** Venice **9.** All's Well That Ends Well, As You Like It, The Comedy of Errors, Cymbeline, Love's Labour's Lost, Measure for Measure, The Merchant of Venice, The Merry Wives of Windsor, A Midsummer Night's Dream, Much Ado About Nothing, Pericles - Prince of Tyre, The Taming of the Shrew, The Tempest, Twelfth Night, The Two Gentlemen of Verona, Troilus & Cressida, The Winter's Tale **10.** Henry V **11.** Claire Danes **12.** Macbeth **13.** Hamlet **14.** Sonnet